Dragon King

Also From Donna Grant

Don't miss these other spellbinding novels!

Dark King Series
Dark Heat (3 novella compilation)
Darkest Flame
Fire Rising
Burning Desire
Hot Blooded
Night's Blaze
Soul Scorched
Dragon King (novella)

Dark Warrior Series
Midnight's Master
Midnight's Lover
Midnight's Seduction
Midnight's Warrior
Midnight's Kiss
Midnight's Captive
Midnight's Temptation
Midnight's Promise
Midnight's Surrender (novella)

Chiasson Series
Wild Fever
Wild Dream
Wild Need
Wild Flame

LaRue Series
Moon Kissed
Moon Thrall

Rogues of Scotland Series
The Craving
The Hunger
The Tempted
The Seduced

Dragon King

A Dark Kings Novella

By Donna Grant

1001 Dark Nights

EVIL EYE
CONCEPTS

Dragon King
A Dark Kings Novella
By Donna Grant

1001 Dark Nights
Copyright 2015 Donna Grant
ISBN: 978-1-940887-67-8

Foreword: Copyright 2014 M. J. Rose
Published by Evil Eye Concepts, Incorporated

Sign up for the 1001 Dark Nights Newsletter
and be entered to win a Tiffany Key necklace.

There's a contest every month!

Go to www.1001DarkNights.com to subscribe!

As a bonus, all subscribers will receive a free
1001 Dark Nights story

The First Night
by Lexi Blake & M.J. Rose

One Thousand and One Dark Nights

Once upon a time, in the future…

*I was a student fascinated with stories and learning.
I studied philosophy, poetry, history, the occult, and
the art and science of love and magic. I had a vast
library at my father's home and collected thousands
of volumes of fantastic tales.*

*I learned all about ancient races and bygone
times. About myths and legends and dreams of all
people through the millennium. And the more I read
the stronger my imagination grew until I discovered
that I was able to travel into the stories… to actually
become part of them.*

*I wish I could say that I listened to my teacher
and respected my gift, as I ought to have. If I had, I
would not be telling you this tale now.
But I was foolhardy and confused, showing off
with bravery.*

*One afternoon, curious about the myth of the
Arabian Nights, I traveled back to ancient Persia to
see for myself if it was true that every day Shahryar
(Persian: شهریار, "king") married a new virgin, and then
sent yesterday's wife to be beheaded. It was written
and I had read, that by the time he met Scheherazade,
the vizier's daughter, he'd killed one thousand
women.*

*Something went wrong with my efforts. I arrived
in the midst of the story and somehow exchanged
places with Scheherazade – a phenomena that had
never occurred before and that still to this day, I
cannot explain.*

Now I am trapped in that ancient past. I have taken on Scheherazade's life and the only way I can protect myself and stay alive is to do what she did to protect herself and stay alive.

Every night the King calls for me and listens as I spin tales. And when the evening ends and dawn breaks, I stop at a point that leaves him breathless and yearning for more. And so the King spares my life for one more day, so that he might hear the rest of my dark tale.

As soon as I finish a story... I begin a new one... like the one that you, dear reader, have before you now.

Chapter One

Grace was screwed. Royally screwed. As in, her career was over. Finished. *Finite.*

She turned on the windshield wipers and slowed the car as she drove through the rain in the mountains. With a renewed grip on the steering wheel, she sent a quick prayer that the rain would stop.

A little sprinkle she could handle. A storm...well, that was another matter entirely.

She puffed out her cheeks as she exhaled. If only she was in Scotland for a holiday, but that wasn't the case at all. In a last-ditch effort to give her muse a good swift kick in the pants, Grace decided to travel to Scotland.

All her friends thought she had lost her mind. Her editor thought it was just one more excuse in a very long line of them as to why she hadn't turned the book in.

Grace wished she knew the reason the words just stopped coming. One day they were there, and the next...gone, vanished. Poof!

Writing wasn't just her career. It was her life. Because within the words and pages she was able to write about heroines who had relationships she would never have. It was the sad truth, but it was the truth.

Grace accepted her lot...in a way. She might realize the string of miserable dates were complete misses and admit that. However, the stories running through her head allowed her to dream as far as she could, and encounter men and adventures sitting behind a computer never would.

Not being able to find the words anymore was like having someone steal her soul.

She breathed a sigh of relief when the rain stopped and she was able to turn off her windshield wipers. In the two hours since she checked into the B&B, it hadn't stopped raining.

Rain was a part of being in Scotland, and she was pushing herself with her fear of storms to be out in it as well. It proved how far she would go to find her soul again. She needed to write, to sink into another world where she could find happiness and a love that lasted forever.

Now she was armed with her laptop and steely determination. She would find her muse again. Just as soon as she found the right place. The scenery along the highway was stunning, but the noise of the passing vehicles would be too much.

Grace needed somewhere off the beaten path. Somewhere she could pretend she was the only person left in the world.

Already three months past due on the book, she felt the pressure to write. Which wasn't helping her creativity in the least. Her editor had already informed her if she didn't turn the book in three weeks from now, then the contract would be canceled.

A full book in three weeks. Yeah, Grace was nothing if not optimistic. She was aiming for having at least half done by then. Perhaps her editor would take mercy on her and allow her to finish the book.

She laughed at her optimism. Based on the last e-mail from her editor, it was either the entire book or nothing. Her entire future and career was on the line.

Grace exited off the highway. She had no idea where she was going. She would know the perfect place when she found it. Narrow roads had her driving slower, which allowed her to take in the sights.

A couple of times she pulled off the road and rolled down her window, but the sounds of civilization could still be heard. So she kept driving deeper and deeper into the mountains.

She didn't worry about getting lost. The GPS on her phone would get her back to the B&B in one piece. No, her entire focus was on finding a place to write.

When drops of rain began to land on the windshield, Grace glanced over at the passenger seat to her rain jacket. All she could hope for was that it remained sprinkling.

If there was a storm, Grace knew her fear would kick in, and she'd be done for. Astraphobia it was called, and it sucked. One wouldn't think there were many storms any given month, right? Except when it was your fear, and it felt as if they followed you around.

No amount of research she'd done on thunder and lightning storms stopped her fear. Just hearing the rumble of thunder sent chills down to the very marrow of her bones. And lightning? She shuddered just thinking about it.

Some thought such awesome displays of nature were beautiful. All Grace could think about was hiding any time lightning zigzagged through the sky. She was in complete flight mode during those storms.

It's why she constantly checked the weather. She rarely got caught unawares anymore, unless a storm cropped up at night. But she wasn't in Los Angeles or Paris right now. She was in Scotland—a country known for its rainfall.

"I'm in a country with daily rainfall while trying to get past my writer's block because of this need to have my story set in Scotland. Oh, yeah. This was a fabulous idea," she told herself while glancing at the sky to see how dark the rainclouds were.

Grace didn't know how long or how far she drove. Taking back roads and roads that weren't roads at all put her further and further from human contact, just as she wanted.

Until she was driving on grass and came to a dead end at the base of a mountain. Grace was about to turn around when she paused. She stared at the jagged peaks and the grass covering the rocks. After a moment, she turned off her engine and opened her door.

The quiet was broken only by the wind and the sounds of birds. Peace. That's what the place emanated. She looked down at her mobile and saw that the service wasn't working.

There was a brief moment of panic when she couldn't check the weather, but then she looked up at the sky. The sun was peaking out of the clouds.

"Just what I need. No noise from the city or constant interruptions. If I'm going to write, I've got to take this chance."

Grace grabbed her laptop and raincoat and got out of the car. She hiked up the mountain about fifty feet before she found a boulder that made a perfect seat.

For several minutes, she simply sat and looked out over the area. Mountains rose up all around before giving way to breathtaking valleys— or glens, as the Scots called them.

Glens were inspiring places that were as unique as each mountain around them. Many of the glens remained unchanged for thousands of years.

Grace spotted a small waterfall that fell into a stream that wound down the mountain and into a valley. The beauty was unmistakable.

It was the first time in ages that Grace felt released, boundless. Unrestricted.

As she watched the clouds move briskly across the sky, she let her mind drift to her book. Excitement flared when she saw a scene play out in her mind.

For so very long, her characters had refused to talk to her, denied to show her anything of their story. But now they had begun to come alive once more.

Grace opened her laptop with the document waiting. She typed as fast as the words came to her. She didn't stop to correct spelling, didn't halt to see if what was happening would work. She simply wrote. Bad pages were easier to fix than blank ones.

The words continued to pour out of her. She became so focused on them that she didn't know how many pages she had written. She went from one chapter to the next, her smile growing bigger and bigger as everything finally began to come together.

It was the first fat drop of water in the middle of her keyboard that halted her. Her heart seized, panic threatening to take hold. But she was finally writing!

Grace's hands were shaking as she looked up to see a rather dark cloud settling above her. This couldn't be happening. Not when she was writing again.

Anger mixed with her dread. She briefly thought of returning to her car. Another drop of rain landed atop her left hand.

The drops were small and coming irregularly. She could retreat as she always did with the rain, or she could try to get past her fear and keep writing.

She stood and looked around, turning in a full circle as she scanned the area for someplace that would shield her from the rain.

"Yes!" Grace said triumphantly as she spotted an overhang of rock from the mountain off to her right. It was just big enough to keep the rain off her.

Grace saved her work and closed her laptop before she began the climb, her heart pounding so hard she thought it might burst from her chest. With every step farther from her car, she knew she was pushing herself all in the name of her story.

The spot wasn't that much higher, but the climb wasn't nearly as smooth. It didn't help that the spattering of rain became a drizzle. She stopped and put on her raincoat, tucking her computer inside to keep it dry.

Several minutes later and out of breath, Grace settled on the grass and opened her computer. Her hands were still shaking, but the rain hadn't increased. She could do this. She could sit through a rain shower and write. As long as there was no thunder and lightning.

She took a deep breath and opened her mind to her characters once more. Surprisingly, it was just as easy to fall back into the story. Grace could hardly believe her luck. If only she had thought to come to Scotland months ago.

To live so close to the very place she set her book and not visit. It was ridiculous, really.

Grace forgot about the past few months as the words flew from her fingers onto the page. Before she knew it, she had written forty-five pages. In one sitting!

She shivered in the cool air and looked up from the screen to see that the rain was beginning to taper off to almost nothing. The overhang kept the water off her, but the steep decline down to her car looked treacherous.

And it wasn't as if Grace had worn the best shoes. Her tennis shoes were adequate for a short stroll, but not for a walk down a rain-soaked mountain.

Grace went back to writing, intending to reach the fifty-page mark. She was on a roll, and nothing was going to stop her now.

* * * *

Arian paced the cavern in his mountain in agitation and a wee bit of anxiety. He was shaking off the dragon sleep from the past six hundred years. Not only had it been six centuries since he had been in human form, but there was a war the Dragon Kings were involved in.

Con and the others were waiting for him to join in the war. Every King had been woken to take part. After all the wars they had been involved in, Arian wasn't happy to be woken to join another.

Because of Ulrik. The banished and disgraced Dragon King hadn't just made a nuisance of himself, but he somehow managed to get his magic returned.

Which meant the Kings needed to put extra magic into keeping the four silver dragons sleeping undisturbed deep within the mountain. They were Ulrik's dragons, and he would want to wake them soon.

But it wasn't just Ulrik that was causing mischief. The Dark Fae were as well. It infuriated Arian that they were once more fighting the Dark. Hadn't the Fae Wars killed enough Fae and dragons?

Then again, as a Dragon King as old as time itself, they were targets for others who wanted to defeat them.

For Ulrik, he just wanted revenge. Arian hated him for it, but he could understand. Mostly because Arian had briefly joined Ulrik in his quest to rid the realm of humans.

Thoughts of Ulrik were pushed aside as Arian found himself thinking about why he had taken to his mountain. When he came here six hundred years earlier, it was to remain there for many thousands of years.

The Dragon Kings sought their mountains for many reasons. Some were just tired of dealing with mortals, but others had something they wished to forget for a while. Arian was one of the latter.

There were many things he did in his past when the King of Kings, Constantine, asked. Not all of them Arian was proud of. The one that sent him to his mountain still preyed upon him.

He didn't remember her name, but he remembered her tears. Because of the spell to prevent any of the Dragon Kings from falling in love with mortals, Arian had easily walked away from the female.

Six centuries later, he could still hear her begging him to stay with her, still see the tears coursing down her face. Though he hadn't felt anything, it bothered him that he had so easily walked away. Because Con had demanded it.

Loyalty—above all else.

The Dragon Kings were his family, and Dreagan his home. There was never any question if he were needed that Arian would do whatever it took to help his brethren in any capacity asked of him.

Arian wasn't angry at himself for choosing loyalty for Dreagan. It was expected. What he had grown tired of was the monotony of his existence.

He halted, a shiver of awareness overtaking him. With his mountain being one of those closest to the border, Arian was attuned to anything that crossed through their dragon magic barrier.

And something significant just crossed onto Dreagan.

Arian shifted into human form. He flexed his fingers several times before fisting his hand. Then he rotated his shoulders. Next he dropped his chin to his chest and rolled his head from one side to the other, stretching muscles that hadn't been used in centuries.

He had no clothes, but then again there wasn't a need for any. Con visited each King who was sleeping every ten years and passed on everything that was going on in the world.

And a lot had happened.

When Darius , another Dragon King, woke him, he informed Arian of the recent happenings regarding the Dark Fae and Ulrik. It could be a

Dark Fae out there, or it could be an MI5 agent.

No way was Arian going to let anyone onto Dreagan—mortal or immortal. They were going to die before they could go a step further.

Arian strode from the cavern through the tunnels in his mountain until he came to the entrance. Before him stood a large pool of water that was as still as glass.

Stalactites hung from the ceiling in various sizes. Only a paltry scrap of light penetrated the thick darkness from the cave entrance.

Arian eyed the opening that was large enough for him to fit through in dragon form. He made his way around the body of water, his feet making nary a sound. Then he paused at the cave entrance.

The world was cast in a gray sheen that made him blink several times for his eyes to adjust. A light smattering of rain fell, wetting everything.

He kept to the shadows of the cave and peered outside where he felt the intruder. Arian spotted a bright orange shoe. What had Con called them when he visited a few years ago? Aye. Tennis shoes.

Arian closed his eyes and used his dragon magic to sense who he would be fighting. Instantly he felt the human. His eyes snapped open. It was going to be an easy fight.

Just as he was about to step outside, the rain began to fall harder. He heard a curse from what sounded like a female. Arian frowned. He didn't like fighting females, but he would do what he had to do.

"Shit. Shit, shit, shit, shittttttttttt," said the distinctly feminine voice with a slight accent to it he couldn't quite place.

There was fear in her tone that stopped him. He stilled as she stood and clumsily began to come closer to the entrance, an entrance she wasn't supposed to be able to see because it was cloaked in dragon magic.

So she had found his cave. It made no difference. She would get no farther than where he was. And…he was going to learn how she was able to see through the magic.

She barreled past him, her back to him as she shook out her blonde locks that stopped at her chin. She raked her hand through her wet hair and sighed loudly, her gaze never leaving the rain.

Visibly shaking, he wasn't sure if it was due to the cold or if she was filled with terror. By the pallor of her skin, he was beginning to think she was frightened.

After several moments, the female relaxed a fraction. It was almost as if she had been waiting for something.

"It's just rain. Only rain." She briefly closed her eyes. "I was making such progress too." She held up a thin rectangle object and spoke to it.

"You better not have gotten wet. I need you."

Arian raised a brow. Was she daft? Or was it some trick to keep him off guard.

She turned around before glancing outside again. Her gaze slid right over him, never seeing him in the shadows. Arian was taken aback by her earthy beauty.

Her creamy skin was flawless. She had large, thick-lashed eyes that were a blue so dark Arian had never seen the like. His gaze raked over her heart-shaped face, from her forehead and slightly arched brows to her high cheekbones, and finally her plump lips.

She hugged the thin object against her and shivered in the green jacket that hid her figure from him. But if her slim legs encased in denim were any indication, he was going to like what he saw beneath.

Her blonde hair was a soft yellow that made him think of daisies bending slightly in the wind. With her locks hanging thick and wet against her damp skin, all Arian could think about was touching her hair, running his fingers through it.

She sighed, drawing his eyes back to her mouth. A mouth that was too seductive by far. The fact he was wondering how her lips would feel against his was a prime indication that the last thing Arian should encounter after six centuries of sleeping was a beautiful woman who made him ache to touch her.

Chapter Two

Grace couldn't believe her luck. It seemed too good to be true to find a place that opened up her creativity and allowed her to get the book written.

Of course, she'd only written fifty pages out of four hundred. That wasn't nearly enough. But it was a great start. If only it hadn't begun raining harder. It was like someone had turned on a faucet. Add in the gusting wind and Grace was quickly soaked.

It was by sheer chance alone that she'd seen the cave. Thankfully, it was close enough that she was able to get to it without too much effort. The fact she'd been able to move through her fear was an improvement.

She opened the laptop and sighed when the screen lit up. With the amount of water that hit her, she'd been worried it had been too much for the computer.

Grace felt her muscles ease as the tension began to subside. Every moment that passed without thunder or lightning made her anxiety diminish.

Then a chill raced down her spine. Slowly, she turned and looked behind her. She suddenly realized that she had no idea how big the cave was. Or if she was the only occupant.

She grabbed her mobile and turned on the flashlight. Her eyes widened as she took in the size of the cavern. The ceiling began just a few feet above her, but the deeper the cave went, the higher the ceiling soared.

Small and insignificant. That's how the cavern made her feel.

The light from her mobile then met the water, and she sucked in a breath. Slowly, she moved the light from one side of the water to the other, noting the expanse of it all.

"Wow," she said in a whisper.

If only she could see it better. The meager light from her phone showed a lot, but not as much as she wanted to see. She wanted to walk around the water, but she hesitated when another chill snaked through her.

The weight of her laptop in her hand reminded her that she should work while she could. Grace turned off the flashlight and pocketed her mobile.

Then she sat her laptop down and removed her raincoat. Once she was seated and leaning back against a rock, she placed her raincoat over her damp jeans for warmth then positioned the computer atop her legs.

A quick check of her watch for the time told her she had been on the mountain for almost three hours. She smiled, happy in all she had accomplished so far. Even with the rain.

In moments she was back to typing, immersed in the story once again. Despite her stomach growling, Grace kept going. The rain couldn't last forever. Could it?

She didn't know what caused her head to jerk up and look to her left. Grace stared into the shadows as she fumbled for her mobile and turned on the flashlight.

A loud sigh escaped her when she saw nothing but rocks. It was her imagination playing tricks on her. With the deafening sound of the rain hitting the rock at the entrance and the quiet of the cave, it was a tad unnerving.

Looking around, she realized just how dark it was in the cave. The light from her laptop made her forget until she looked up from the screen.

Grace saved her progress after she saw she had now written another ten pages. Maybe it was a good thing she was stuck on the mountain. It was obviously just what she needed to write.

Please no thunder and lightning.

She closed the laptop to save battery and stretched her arms over her head. Her pants were drying, but still damp. How she hated wearing wet jeans.

The dampness from the cave was beginning to sink into her. Grace put on her raincoat and got to her feet. She walked to the entrance and looked out.

The rain hadn't slacked off at all. If anything, it looked like it was coming down even heavier. She leaned out to see if she could spot her car, but she didn't have any luck.

She was well and truly stuck until the rain stopped. Grace wrapped her arms around herself. Her stomach soured as she imagined a thunderstorm rolling in.

"Please no," she mumbled.

At least she wasn't without resources. She might be hungry and thirsty, but she had a source of water behind her. Not to mention she still had plenty of battery on her laptop to get more writing done.

That is if she could with the rain continuing. She was doing all right in the day, but at night? That was another matter entirely.

The only thing that made her worry was if she had to stay overnight. It wasn't that Grace minded sleeping on the ground. In fact, she loved to camp. Never mind that it had been over twelve years since she had done it.

Sleeping bag or not, she would be fine if she was forced to have an overnight visit in the cave—as long as it stopped raining. And things could definitely be worse. She could be outside in the weather.

Or it could be thundering.

Or someone could be in the cave with her.

Grace chuckled to herself. A heartbeat later the hairs on the back of her neck stood on end. She whirled around. Someone was there. She knew it. She might not be able to see them or hear them, but it was an instinct she couldn't ignore.

Unless...it wasn't a person at all. It could be an animal.

Which didn't make her feel any better about the situation.

Grace turned on the flashlight on her phone again. She walked far enough from the entrance so that she could hear. Halting next to the rock where she had been writing, Grace slowly moved the light from one side of the cave to the other. She pointed it specifically into the areas with the most shadows.

She was just about to turn it off when she felt a presence behind her. Grace stilled, her heart jumping into her throat.

"What are you doing here, lass?" asked a deep, masculine voice with a thick Scot's accent.

Grace whirled around. His face was hidden by the light from the entrance behind him. He was so tall she had to look up at him. And if he was trying to intimidate her, he succeeded without much effort at all. The shadows hid him almost completely. "Who are you?"

"It doesna matter. You're on private property."

She blinked, wondering if she could reach the entrance before he could grab her. That would put her out in the rain, but it was either that or deal with a crazy man. Damn, but she hated her options.

Grace decided to take another approach. Truth and meekness. It might buy her enough time to get away. "I didn't know."

"You expect me to believe that?"

Well, hell. Could his voice be any sexier? It had a rough edge to it. As if he hadn't used it in a very long while. And why did she yearn to see his face? It shouldn't matter if he was as gorgeous as his voice.

Yes, it does.

"I do expect you to believe me," she stated. "I'm not from here."

"Aye. I gather that from your accent."

There was no denying he wasn't happy she was in the cave. As intimidated as his size made her feel, she didn't feel threatened. Odd. Very odd.

Grace pointed outside. "Have you seen the rain? If I go out in that now, I could fall to my death."

"How did you get inside?"

At this she nearly laughed. "Um...well, I saw the entrance and walked in."

"How did you see it?"

Was he for real? Was he messing with her or high on some drugs? "With my eyes."

"You shouldna have come here."

"Here?" she asked as she looked around, her arms out to her sides. "Where is here?"

She could almost feel him raising a brow at her. Oh, if only she could see his face!

"As if you doona know," he replied acerbically.

Grace crossed her arms in front of her chest and gave him the best glare she had. It was more than difficult, especially when she happened to glance at his chest and noticed that he wasn't wearing a shirt.

All Grace could see was his right shoulder all the way to his neck, where his long hair came into view. Even with just a hint of light from the entrance, she could ascertain that his hair was very dark. Black? Or dark brown? Hard to determine.

She could tell it was long, but the shadows kept her from seeing where the ends were. Never had Grace encountered a man with such hair. It should make him appear feminine looking, but even from the partial silhouette and his voice, he was anything but.

It was then she realized she had been staring. Grace lifted her chin. "I don't know where I am. Why can't you believe me?"

He chuckled, but it held no mirth. His head then tilted to the side and she saw more of his hair fall over his very wide, very thick shoulders.

Something stirred within her, as if the longer she looked at him the more aware she became. Every time he breathed she noticed how his chest expanded. With just the slightest movement, his long locks moved.

Was it wrong that she wanted to sink her hands in his length and press against him?

"I doona know you," he replied.

It took her a second to realize he was speaking. Then it dawned on Grace that she shouldn't be getting angry with him. She dropped her arms to her side and pointed to her laptop. "I came to Scotland to write. You see, I'm desperately behind on my deadline, and I must finish. I found this mountain and its beauty. I'm able to write here. Please, allow me to stay during the day and write. I'll be happy to pay for that privilege."

She waited for him to scoff at her words. Instead, there was only silence.

Grace shifted uncomfortably under his gaze. He had full view of her where she could only see one shoulder. Granted, she could make out the detail of corded muscle, but it still wasn't enough. She couldn't see his face or read his expressions.

"Nay. You need to leave."

She opened her mouth in shock. "Leave? Have you looked outside? I can't leave in this!"

She wouldn't. It was raining, and where there was rain, there were thunder and lightning. Not happening. She shook her head to prove her point, even if he didn't know her inner monologue.

"Sure you can. Pick your way slowly down the mountain. You can no' remain here."

Grace snorted in disbelief. "I thought Scottish men were chivalrous. Apparently, I was misinformed. I'm not about to go out there and fall to my death just because you're being stubborn."

Long, strong fingers wrapped around her arms and lifted her to her tiptoes. She could feel the power in those hands, could sense the barely leashed animal inside him.

Yet, his hold was strangely gentle.

"You need to leave," he stated. "Now."

She glanced outside and saw that the rain had stopped. How...odd. If she didn't know better, she'd think he turned it off just by wishing it so. Which was ludicrous. No one could do that.

"Fine. I'll leave. You might've just sealed my fate as far as my career goes, but I'll leave your mountain."

Did she hear him snigger? That only infuriated Grace all the more. She grabbed her laptop and stalked to the entrance. He wasn't even going to let the sun dry some of the water on the mountain. But she'd be damned if she fell and gave him something else to laugh at.

Grace was at the entrance to the cave. She took one step out when she looked down the mountain and spotted four men running toward her.

Good. Maybe they would be more gallant and at least help her to her car. She lifted her hand to wave to them. Her arm didn't rise farther than her face when she was hastily jerked back into the cave and pressed against a stone wall...and a solid wall of muscle.

Her mouth went dry as her free hand landed on his stomach. She could feel every breath he took, every ripple of his hard muscle.

"Doona move," he whispered urgently.

First, he wanted her to leave. Now he wanted her to stay. What was going on? Not that she could think straight with his body against hers.

She lifted her gaze and felt her breath catch. His face was turned toward the opening as he stared with a severe look in his eyes.

His face seemed to have been cut from the very granite at her back. The hard planes and angles would be too harsh on some men. But not him. He was breathtakingly striking, astonishingly magnificent.

Her hand flattened on his abdomen to feel more of him while she wished she wasn't holding her laptop so her other hand could be touching him as well.

Then his head slowly turned to look down at her. She could scarcely believe the light-goldish hue of his eyes. They reminded her of the champagne she had drunk the night before.

His hair was as black as midnight and hung to the middle of his back. His forehead was high, his nose straight. He had thick black brows that slashed over his intense eyes. His lips, wide and full, turned up slightly at one corner.

His eyes met hers, as if daring her to look at him. Grace let her hand lower to his hip, and she had another shock as she discovered him naked.

Now those lips of his turned up in a full smile. He liked that he had surprised her.

And she kinda liked it to. After all, when was the last time that had happened?

"I..." She cleared her throat and tried again. "I thought you wanted me to leave."

His smile vanished in an instant. "That time is gone."

Something in his words sent up a warning in her brain. "What's that mean?"

"It means you'll get to write your book."

He took a step back from her the same time a bolt of lightning zigzagged across the sky and thunder rumbled. A second later, the skies opened up again.

Chapter Three

Arian wasn't certain whether to believe the mortal. She could very well be with the Dark Fae rapidly approaching his cave.

With a wave of his hand, Arian cloaked the entrance with more dragon magic. No one was supposed to be able to find the cave except another King. Still, the fact the Dark knew which side of the mountain was his cave was enough to cause him alarm.

"I really don't like being ordered about," the female said in a sassy tone as she looked worriedly to the entrance. She tried to move away, but he wouldn't let her.

He had always thought the American drawl was a bit too rough of all the accents Con had shown him through his dragon sleep. But rolling off her tongue, Arian found he quite liked it. He heard another accent as well, though he couldn't pinpoint it.

"You wanted to stay here, did you no'?" he asked as he took another step away from her.

"I'm getting whiplash you change your mind so quickly," she said, her gaze pinning him. Then a crack of thunder filled the silence, causing her to visibly cringe. "Those men could've helped me. I'd be off your mountain and out of your hair."

He glanced out the cave. "As tempting as that offer sounds, you're going to remain."

"Yeah. That sounds good."

"Because I doona trust you." It took him a moment to realize she hadn't asked why as he expected. Arian frowned when he saw she had her arms wrapped around herself while she inched farther away from the opening.

The war the Dragon Kings were in meant that everyone was a potential enemy. The only way they were going to come out of this as secret as before was if every Dragon King assumed one and all was an enemy until they proved otherwise.

And the American had a lot to prove.

"Yep," she said with a nod. "Perfectly understandable. Trust is...trust is... Oh, hell. Nevermind," she mumbled.

Arian glanced at the rain when lightning struck, and she hastily turned away. The way she was breathing shallowly and a fine sheen of sweat covered her were classic symptoms of someone who was terrified.

She looked like at any moment she was going to fall apart, and that's one thing Arian didn't want. A crying female was...well, they were the worst kind of hell for a man—or dragon—to endure. If he could bypass her tears, then he'd consider it a win.

"Perhaps you should leave. It's just a wee bit of rain."

Her navy eyes jerked to him, widening just enough in her outrage. "Not happening."

She pushed away from the wall, her gaze raking down his body as she walked past him, her fear seemingly forgotten in her anger. That scathing look roused him, stirred him.

His balls tightened and his blood heated. Six centuries was a long time to go without relieving his body, and he was feeling the effects of that abstinence profoundly.

The mortal's body was more than adequate. He had the pleasure of seeing—and feeling—more of her. In fact, he found her curves rather enticing. Even the fire in her eyes did something to him.

Arian knew lust well. Aye, he lusted for her greatly. Yet there was something else he couldn't name. Was it because he had watched her fingers punch the keys on her laptop and the words form? Was it because she was scared of him and still had the gumption to stand up to him?

Or was it something else?

Her gaze on him, however, sent all the blood straight to his cock. Arian turned to keep that part of himself in shadow. He didn't want her to know how much a look from her could do to him.

He covertly watched as she returned to her spot near the boulder that stood unmovable about ten feet from the water. She opened the laptop, the light highlighting her face. She blinked quickly before she sat her fingers on the keys. A heartbeat later, she was writing again.

Arian toned down the thunder and lightning. Every Dragon King had a special power, and his was controlling the weather. When he saw her shoulders begin to relax once more, Arian had confirmation that it was storms Grace was frightened of.

While she had been working the first time, he had come up behind the boulder and read over her shoulder. She was really quite good, and he wanted to know how the story progressed. It wasn't just her way with words, but it was how she described things that made Arian feel as if he were in the middle of the story.

In ancient mortal times, she would've been revered for her gifts. And yet, she appeared as if she carried the weight of the world on her shoulders. Then he remembered how she made a comment about needing to finish the book.

"You're not going to stand there and watch me, are you?" she asked with a sigh.

Arian turned his back to her and moved closer to the entrance. The Dark continued to search the mountain for the entrance. How long could he hold them off? The mortal wasn't a Druid, but that didn't mean she wasn't a decoy of some kind.

"It's Grace, by the way."

He frowned and turned his head to the side. "Excuse me?"

"My name. I knew you were about to ask, so I saved you the trouble."

He hid his smile because he liked her sass. Grace. Aye, the name suited her.

"And yours?"

He looked at her over his shoulder. "Arian."

"Arian," she said, letting it roll off her tongue slowly.

His balls tightened again. Damn but she was a distraction he didn't want. Arian needed to get to Dreagan Manor with the other Kings, but with the Dark having arrived, he was glad he remained.

There was a push on his mind. Arian opened the mental link between Dragon Kings and heard Con's voice ask, *"Our barrier was breached near you twice."*

"Aye. It was a mortal woman the first time."

"Did you send her on her way?"

"Was about to when four Dark arrived," Arian explained.

Con let out a string of curses. *"Is the female with them?"*

"I'm no' sure. Yet."

"*I'm sending Tristan and Banan to lead the Dark away from you.*"

Arian looked at the mortal. "*And I'll figure out what the human really wants.*"

"*Doona take too long. You're needed here,*" Con stated before he severed the link.

Grace was staring at him again. "Do you always walk around naked?"

"Does it bother you, lass?" Arian asked with a grin.

"Of course not. I'm not a prude."

He turned away so she wouldn't see his smile. Arian had the overwhelming urge to goad her, and he didn't hold back. "Do you no' like what you see?"

"I...yes. You have a nice body."

"Nice," Arian said with a shrug. He glanced at her. "Nice isna that good."

She looked down at the laptop and pressed her lips together. "Fine. I'll admit it's more than nice. It's...very nice. Gorgeous even."

Was she blushing? Arian couldn't look away. She said the words, but she wouldn't meet his gaze. How...enchanting.

Grace shrugged and punched a few keys on her laptop. "You asked."

"So I did."

She peeked up at him before she focused on the screen. Its white light highlighted her face as she began typing. He made himself turn away before he continued their banter—which he was enjoying entirely too much.

Arian's gaze was focused outside. The Dark were still there, and he couldn't help but wonder why Grace hadn't asked about them again. Could it be that she wasn't with them? It was a slim chance. Most likely she didn't mention them again because she was working with them.

And Arian didn't like that thought at all. He enjoyed Grace. Her accent, her feisty nature, her beauty, and her intellect intrigued him. Not to mention her ability to craft a story. In all his years—and they were endless—he hadn't met anyone like her.

Arian surreptitiously looked at her. She seemed absorbed in her work. Her brow was furrowed slightly one moment, and a second before she was smiling at whatever she was typing. How he wanted to know what amused her.

It was the sound of dragon wings that pulled his attention from her. Tristan and Banan arrived quietly, dropping from the sky with wings tucked as they zeroed in on the Dark Fae.

Banan's deep blue claws grabbed a Dark before they were even seen.

Tristan opened his amber-colored wings and circled around the group of Dark.

Arian craved to be out there with them. He actually had to stop himself from shifting and joining in the fight, the instinct was so great. But he wasn't about to leave Grace.

Not until he learned if she had wandered into his mountain on accident or not.

If she was innocent, then she didn't need to see the battle taking place on the side of his mountain.

Arian fisted his hands at his sides as he struggled not to join the fight. He needed to be there, wiping the Dark from his mountain instead of standing there watching.

The Dark threw bubbles of magic at Tristan and Banan. Many they were able to dodge, but a few magic balls found their mark.

Arian knew how painful Dark magic could be. He clenched his jaw and struggled to remain in his cave as Tristan and Banan led the Dark away.

Only when the Dark were out of sight did Arian turn back to Grace. A small frown furrowed her brow as she stared at the computer screen. Her fingers rested on the keyboard, but she was no longer typing.

She closed her eyes and took a deep breath before slowly releasing it. When her lids opened, she typed a few words and then halted once more.

"What is it?" he asked, curious.

She slammed the laptop closed and dropped her head back against the rock. "I don't know."

"I hear another accent in your words besides American. What is it?"

Her head rolled to the side to look at him. "French. My mother is from Paris."

"You doona sound like someone who has lived their life in Paris."

"Because I didn't." She set the laptop beside her and pulled her knees up to her chest. "My father raised me after my mom ran off with a musician. She lived in London for a few years until that relationship ended. Then she returned to Paris."

"She left you behind?" Arian could scarcely imagine such a scenario.

Grace gave a half-snort, half-laugh. "She did. She was in love and didn't want a five-year-old getting in the way."

"I doona ken such a thing."

She rested her chin on her knees. "Me either, but she told me that some people just weren't cut out to be parents. She was one of them. It's a poor excuse, I know."

"Aye. It is."

Grace's deep blue eyes focused on him. "I've spent the last three years living in Paris. My father wanted me to see the world."

"Yet, you remained in Paris instead of returning to him."

"He died. It was the last thing he made me promise. To see the world." She smiled, as if recalling the memory. "We'd been planning the trip for some time, so all the destinations were chosen and everything paid for. The only difference was that I traveled it alone."

Arian moved closer to her. "I'm sorry."

She shrugged and blinked rapidly. "It's all right. Our plan was always to end in Paris so I could spend some time with my mother. I'd already arranged to spend a month in Paris, and after that, I found I liked it."

"So you remained. Did you see your mother?"

Grace chuckled softly. "A bit. She really isn't cut out for parenting. She doesn't have a maternal bone in her body. She had a new man, so I urged her to go with him."

"That was nice."

"Not at all," Grace replied with a laugh. "It was selfish. I didn't want her around either at that point."

Arian found himself smiling. "Who are you, Grace? What are you doing in my mountain?"

She let out a deep breath. "I'm Grace Clark from Los Angeles, California. I'm a writer...er...novelist who lives in Paris."

"What do you write, Grace Clark?"

"Romance novels."

He raised a brow, intrigued. "Interesting."

"It would be if I could get the book written. I turned in the first book of the three-book contract, but I'm beyond late with this second book. If I don't turn it in three weeks from now, they're canceling the rest of my contract."

Arian wasn't sure what all of that meant, but it didn't sound good. "And being here does what?"

"Puts my groove back on."

He might know current events thanks to Con and Darius, but there was obviously still quite a bit Arian needed to catch up on, because he had no idea what she meant.

Grace laughed. "I had writer's block. For some reason, being on this mountain I've written over sixty pages today alone. I've never written that many pages in one sitting. If I can keep this up, I'll meet my deadline."

"It sounds to me, lass, as if there are underlying issues to this writer's block you speak of."

Her eyes fell to the ground. "I'll face that when I get this book turned in. Until then, I must focus." Her gaze returned to him. "So does that mean you'll allow me to stay and write?"

With the Dark gone, there was no reason to keep Grace in the mountain. Arian was relatively certain she wasn't a spy, but then again, she could be a really good mole and actress.

This was going to require him to spend more time with Grace Clark from Los Angeles, California and Paris, France.

"For a wee bit."

Grace's smile was wide as she bestowed it on him. "You're amazing. Thank you so much. This is going to save my ass big time. As soon as it quits raining, I'll leave for the night and return in the morning."

Arian nodded as she spoke, because there was no way he was allowing her to leave. He would make sure the rain continued to keep her trapped.

The only problem was that he was going to have to think about food for her. And light. Because night was approaching quickly.

Arian looked down at himself. And perhaps some clothes as well.

Chapter Four

Grace couldn't write knowing that Arian was watching her. He made her uncomfortable. Not in an "oh my God, he's going to kill me" vibe, but an "I can't look away from that face and body" thing. She would have to be blind not to see how gorgeous he was, even in the dim light of the cave.

A light that was fast fading.

She was thankful that the lightning and thunder had stopped. It hadn't been until she was deep in the story that she realized she had been so caught up in Arian's change of mind for a third time that she had forgotten the storm.

That was a first, to be sure.

Grace checked her battery on the laptop. Fortunately, she had fully charged it the night before. It would last her a few more hours yet, but then what?

"Is something wrong?" Arian asked.

She closed her eyes at the sound of his brogue. How she used to roll her eyes at women who said a man's accent could make them climax. Well, now she knew how true that statement was.

"Grace?"

She bit back a moan. He had to stop saying her name. By all that was holy, didn't he know what it did to her? It was too much. That voice, that accent, *and* her name?

"Are you in pain?"

Her eyes snapped open when she found him squatting in front of her. It was unfortunate that her laptop hid the lower part of him.

She felt her cheeks heat as she pictured him naked in her head. "No. No, I'm fine," she hastily said.

"You didna answer me, lass."

She tried to swallow, but all the moisture in her body seemed to be centered between her legs. "I was thinking."

"Ahh," he said with a nod. "About your book?"

Grace grasped the out he gave her. "That's right. About my book."

She really needed to pull it together. There was no telling how long she would be in the cave with him. Her stomach chose that moment to growl loudly.

His sexy smile did her in. "I was about to ask if you were ready to eat."

"Eat? As in you have food?" she asked hopefully.

He chuckled and stood. That's when she saw he now wore a pair of jeans. Grace saw him walk off, wondering where his shirt and shoes were. Not that she minded him shirtless.

"Of course I have food."

"Of course," she mumbled grumpily to herself as she stood. "Why didn't I think to ask for it earlier."

When she followed him, she found him staring at her. The light from outside was fading, so she was only able to make out his raised brow.

"Sorry," she said with a wince. "I tend to get obnoxious when I'm hungry."

"Then I'll make sure you have plenty of food."

There was a click and light flooded the area from an electric lantern set by the water. Grace looked around in awe before turning back to Arian. She stared into his champagne eyes and forgot to breath. It was wrong for someone to be so handsome that he made all thought vanish.

"Choose whatever you'd like," Arian said.

Grace pulled her gaze from him and looked down where there was a basket of food perched on a boulder that came almost to her waist. And good food like roasted chicken, several kinds of cheese, bread, water, and even a bottle of wine.

She glanced up at him and asked, "This looks like a picnic basket. I hope I didn't interrupt anything with you and your woman."

"I doona have a woman. I bring food with me when I doona know how long I'll be staying."

The words sounded right, but there was just something that didn't sit well with her. Grace studied him, wondering if she could believe him. It wasn't like she had much choice. She was stuck in a cave with him while the next great flood was happening outside.

And he had food.

Grace grabbed a chicken wing, a piece of bread, and water. She stood beside the basket and began to eat, snagging a piece of cheese every few bites.

She wasn't the only one. Arian was also eating as he stood on the other side of the basket. She could feel his gaze on her, but Grace didn't care. She was starving.

"When was the last time you ate, lass?"

Grace took a long drink of water before she said, "This morning when I reached the B&B where I'm staying."

"You should've brought food with you."

"I should've. Then again, I didn't realize the storm of the century was going to happen today and that I'd get stuck in a cave."

He smiled and took a bite of chicken. "Why did you choose this mountain?"

"It was by chance."

"Tell me," he urged.

Grace finished chewing. "Coming to Scotland was my last-ditch effort to get the story written. I've tried everything conceivable that other authors have attempted to break past their writer's block. Nothing worked."

"So you came here."

"I'd been two years earlier and loved it. I thought perhaps if I returned that it might get me writing. I headed out this morning looking for a place that was quiet and beautiful."

Arian's head cocked to the side, allowing several thick strands of black hair to fall over his shoulder. "There are no roads leading here."

"I know." Grace laughed and shook her head at her foolishness. "I decided to find my perfect place I needed to get off the beaten path, so to speak. I took the first road I found. Then I turned off that onto a narrower one. Again and again I did that until I came to a dirt road. I traveled that for a long while, veering different directions at times until I ended up here. To be honest, I'm hoping I can find my way back."

"You will."

He said it with such authority that Grace believed him. She finished off her chicken wing and found a second.

"What brought you to this area of Scotland?" he asked.

Grace was beginning to feel like he was questioning her for something. The queries were worded innocently enough, but they all focused on one thing—this mountain.

"I was here before and liked it," she replied.

He nodded, though his gaze didn't leave her. "A simple enough explanation."

"But you don't believe me? Is that it?"

Arian shrugged and reached for the wine. She watched the play of his muscles as he opened the bottle and held up a glass, silently asking her if she wanted some.

Grace gave a shake of her head. "Look, I don't like games of any sort. Well, that's not true. I love backgammon, but my point is that if you want to ask me something, then just ask it. Stop beating around the bush."

"I want to know why you're on my mountain," he said then took a drink of the red wine.

She popped the last bite of cheese and bread in her mouth and chewed while she observed him. Arian was much too confident. He had been naked earlier, but somehow he managed to find a pair of jeans.

Why hadn't he worn them earlier? And why hadn't it bothered her more that he was naked? She should've been screaming, or at the very least wondering about rape. But she had never thought that about him.

He frightened her, yes. But it was with a feeling that he was protecting something, and as long as it remained protected, he wouldn't unleash his anger.

Grace finished her water and wiped her mouth with the back of her hand. She screwed the cap back on the now empty bottle and placed it inside the basket. "I told you why I'm here. I have no more explanation than that."

"I'm afraid that isna enough."

Wasn't enough? Enough for what? Grace frowned and looked toward the cave entrance. Dusk had fallen. She could just make out the shapes of the trees on the opposite mountain. "Where are the men from earlier?"

"Gone."

She slid her gaze back to him. "Gone where?"

"I'm no' sure. They were no' good men. They would've hurt you."

Grace gave a bark of laughter. "You expect me to take your word about that when you refuse to believe anything I say? Oh, that's rich."

"I knew those men. They were no' good men," he repeated.

"And you are?"

He glanced away. "I didna say that. Though I am better than they are."

"What did those men want?"

"Something in these mountains."

Grace immediately had an idea for her next book. "Really? Like what?" she asked excitedly.

It was the uncertain look on Arian's face that made her realize she had been a bit overzealous.

So Grace tried again. "It gave me an idea for a book is all. Your theories for what those men were looking for could help me decide what I have in my book."

"I doona know what they're looking for," Arian said. "They're trespassers."

"This is your land?"

He lifted one shoulder as an answer.

Grace pinned him with a look. "You expect me to answer your questions. It's only fair that you answer mine."

"That's no' how it works, lass. You're on my land. Uninvited, I might add."

"So what? I'm your prisoner?" she asked in shocked anger.

Arian pointed outside to the rain that still fell. "I'm no' keeping you here. The weather is."

"It'd be just my luck that you control the damn weather."

When he didn't so much as bat an eye, Grace began to wonder if he was. Then she laughed at herself. Being back in the Highlands where the people were superstitious seemed to have rubbed off on her as well.

She laughed. "Thanks for the food. I feel much better."

"Of course."

She was still chuckling at herself when she went back to the boulder where she had been writing. Her characters were nestled in a nice hotel in Inverness while it rained. Real life always fell into her stories, and with the constant rain, of course it was part of her plot.

It also allowed lots of time for her hero and heroine to get to spend time together—in and out of bed.

Grace immediately thought of Arian kissing her. Her stomach flipped wildly.

No, she told herself. She wouldn't think of him that way. He was as gorgeous as sin and had a voice as seductive as silk, but it wouldn't do her any good to pine for a man like him.

They had been together for a few hours. If he found her attractive, he would've said something. And Grace had dealt with enough men to know she wasn't going to put herself out there and be rejected. She had a book to write.

At that thought, she cleared her throat and sat before opening her laptop.

After another hour of writing, the words on the screen began to blur. She was mentally tapped out. A quick save of her document, and she turned off the laptop.

Grace heard the crackle before she saw the fire. She found the fire blazing about five feet from the water near where they had eaten.

She saw no sign of Arian, but that didn't worry her. There was only so far he could go in a cave. As she walked to the fire, she saw several tunnels beyond the water that she hadn't spotted earlier because the light from her phone hadn't penetrated the darkness.

But with the fire and the two electronic lanterns set up, she was able to get a good view of the cave. She sat next to the fire and closed her eyes. It felt wonderful to feel the heat penetrating her clothes.

She hadn't realized how cold she had been until she felt the warmth. Now she wished she had a thick blanket and a mug of coffee. And a comfortable chair.

Grace found herself drifting to sleep. So she curled up on her side with her arm beneath her head. Her eyes hurt from staring at the computer screen for so long, and her brain was complete mush after so many pages.

She drifted in thought as she listened to the sounds around her. The splash of rain onto the rock at the entrance, and the stillness within the cave.

At one point, she thought she heard the lap of water near her, but she was too exhausted to open her eyes. She tried to tell herself to remain awake until Arian returned.

Her trusting nature had gotten her into trouble on many occasions, and yet she still freely gave her trust. With her active imagination, she thought of all the things Arian could do to hurt her.

Then she realized, if he had wanted to harm her, he could've done it hours ago.

Arian. Who was he? Why had he been naked? And what was so important about his mountain?

Grace was going to find out. Right after she woke up.

Chapter Five

Arian emerged from the tunnel to find Grace on her side asleep. He had been watching her. It's all he seemed to do since she walked into his cave.

He found it fascinating how she could stare at the computer screen while her fingers flew over the keys as if they had a life of their own. And somehow, a story came from all of it.

Arian had never been any kind of storyteller. It was amazing to him that people could craft such tales.

It also didn't help that he wanted to believe she just stumbled upon his mountain. Earlier, while she worked, Arian had contacted Ryder, a Dragon King with a craving for jelly-filled donuts and a knack for computers.

Ryder confirmed who Grace was as well as her story. Still, that didn't mean she wasn't working for the Dark or Ulrik. Nor did it mean that she was.

Arian walked past her to the entrance and looked out. With a mere thought, he halted the rain. Grace had no idea the rain was situated atop them. Nor did she know how right she was that he could control the weather.

He didn't like to use his powers that way, but there were instances where it was needed. And today had been one of them.

Had he left his cave the day before as Darius urged, Arian wouldn't have been there when Grace arrived. He would've arrived soon after, but he doubted it would have been in time to stop the Dark from finding her or his cave.

Tristan and Banan had killed the Dark hours ago, but it still bothered Arian that they had gotten onto Dreagan. Even fortifying the magic on the perimeter of sixty thousand acres wasn't going to be enough.

The Dark were determined enough to push through the invisible barrier despite great pain to themselves. All because of some weapon the Kings had.

A weapon Con hadn't bothered to tell anyone about.

Arian suspected he was one of the few Kings who didn't mind that Con kept such a secret. It would've been nice to know, but the fact Con hadn't breathed a word of it told Arian it was for a reason. And not just because this weapon could be used to destroy the Kings.

There was something else at play here. Something that no one had thought of. Arian knew it was pointless to ask Con. The King of Kings wouldn't divulge anything he didn't want others to know.

As tight-lipped as he was in regards to the weapon, Con wouldn't be telling anyone anything. Speaking of secrets, Kellan knew a great many as Keeper of the History. He had yet to tell a single one.

Arian stepped out of his mountain and lifted his face to the sky. It had been so long since he had seen the moon. As he looked, he spotted dragons flying among the clouds.

He glanced over his shoulder at Grace, and without another thought, hastily removed his jeans. He leapt into the air, shifting as he did.

His giant turquoise wings stretched outward, catching the air and taking him higher. The beat of dragon wings was all around him. He soared higher into the clouds to his brethren, twisting and turning as he remembered what it was to be a dragon again.

The more he flew, the more he missed his dragons. It was a hollow ache in his chest as he recalled the time before humans. Everything changed with the mortals' arrival. That was the one constant throughout time, and yet he never thought he would see the day that dragons weren't in the sky.

Arian usually didn't fly so close to his mountain for fear of mortals seeing him since he was so near to the Dreagan border. But Grace was inside sleeping. He didn't want to be too far away. Not that anything was going to happen, but he wanted to be prepared.

He gave a nod to Nikolai and Dmitri before he dropped his right wing and circled back toward his mountain. The others would remain until dawn, which was only a few hours away. Arian wanted to stay with them. And he would just as soon as Grace Clark was on her way home.

While flying, Arian had decided to let Grace go. Even if she was working for Ulrik or the Dark, she learned nothing from him. Nor would she. And the sooner she was gone the better.

One of the first things he would do was make damn sure she could never find her way back to the mountain again. Her or anyone, for that matter.

The first ray of sunshine crested the peaks. Arian saw his mountain and was getting ready to shift back into human form when he was alerted that Dark had crossed the border once more.

He flew faster when he spotted them on his mountain for a second time. How were they continuing to get in? He'd find that out later. Right now, his concern was getting rid of them.

Arian opened his mental link and told the other Kings there were two Dark that he was taking care of. If any of the other Kings came, it would likely wake Grace. Arian didn't want her seeing anything.

He tucked his wings and dove. Then he stretched out his wings and opened his talons. He managed to grab one of the Dark, but not the other.

Arian crushed the Dark with his talons and tossed him in the air where he let loose a blast of dragon fire. Ash was all that was left of the Fae.

A volley of Dark magic hit Arian. He turned and flew back to his mountain. The Dark was close to the entrance. Too close, actually.

Did they know that there were tunnels deep below the mountains connecting some of them? Was that why they were resolute to get into his mountain?

Arian landed on the side of the mountain with his wings spread as he stared down at the Dark. He took a deep breath, ready to release another round of fire when he spotted something out of the corner of his eye.

It was Grace.

* * * *

Grace knew her knees were going to give out at any moment. She didn't recall why she had woken, only that she had. With the rain no longer falling, she wanted to see how wet it was. Only she saw two men climbing the mountain.

The next thing she knew, a large form dropped from the sky, only to go back up again the next moment. She gaped in horror when she saw the turquoise dragon burn one of the men.

Before that truly registered in her mind, things got stranger. The remaining man threw what looked like a large bubble at the dragon.

"What the hell," she murmured.

Was she really seeing a dragon? A massive beast that was as beautiful to behold as it was terrifying.

"Dragons aren't real. And yet, there's one. Right there. Right in front of me."

More bubbles hit the dragon. It must've hurt because the dragon spun around and flew back to the man.

Only to land on the side of the mountain.

Grace gawked at the immense width and breadth of the dragon's turquoise wings as he spread them out. The scales fairly gleamed in the morning sun, shining brilliantly like metal.

The dragon had two short brow horns and another short horn atop its nose. The head and body were so huge she could barely grasp it, and the tail extended far behind the dragon, twitching as if waiting to be used as a weapon.

Suddenly, the dragon's black eyes turned to her. She froze in fear, unable to move. The last thing she wanted was to bring the dragon's attention to her. She didn't want to get eaten.

What was that old expression? Don't anger a dragon because you are crunchy.

Well, she didn't want to anger this dragon. She just wanted to go back to the B&B, get some sleep, and then check herself into a mental institution because she was obviously losing her mind if she was seeing dragons.

The dragon's head snapped back to the man, a low rumble coming from its chest. Grace told herself to go back inside the cave and find Arian, but she still couldn't move.

Whether it was from fear or curiosity, she wasn't sure.

But she remained to see what would happen. And as the man began to throw more bubbles at the dragon, she was glad she did.

The dragon was a large target. Even when the dragon knocked the man sideways with its wing, he got back on his feet. As the sun rose higher, Grace got a better look at the man. His short black hair was liberally laced with thick, silver strands.

Everything was odd about the entire scene, from the man to the dragon. It had to be a dream. There was no other explanation for such things.

The man blasted the dragon with several bubbles in a row, and to her shock, Grace watched the dragon disappear in a blink. And in its place was none other than Arian.

He pushed up on his hands and glared at the man. "You're going to die here."

"Not before I find what I'm looking for," replied the man in an Irish accent.

Grace rubbed her eyes. When she opened them and Arian still stood there as naked as she had found him the day before, she wasn't sure what to do.

Then it didn't matter as he and the other man began to attack each other. The fight was vicious in both sight and sound. Arian hit the man hard while more bubbles barreled into Arian.

Then Arian fell to one knee with burns covering his body where the bubbles hit him. Grace covered her mouth with her hand. The shock of seeing him so wounded turned her stomach, but it also made her angry. Who was the man to attack Arian so?

The wounds looked extremely painful. By the way Arian grimaced, they were.

She silently urged him to get up and keep fighting. The fact he was the dragon was something she would face later. She instinctively knew that whoever Arian was fighting wasn't a good person.

The stranger threw another bubble at Arian that caused him to growl in fury. Grace took a step back when she saw the wrath on Arian's face.

He got to his feet and attacked the man again while Grace watched. They were locked together with more bubbles hitting Arian at very close range.

Grace couldn't tell who was winning as the two of them fell together and rolled. For long moments she waited to hear or see something. When nothing happened, Grace walked out of the cave and looked down to find them.

She spotted the black and silver haired man lying face down, unmoving. Arian was on his side with his back to her. And he wasn't moving either.

"Arian," she whispered, worried for him.

Grace briefly thought of getting her laptop and running far away. There was something strange going on at this mountain, and it would be better if she wasn't involved.

But she couldn't leave Arian. He was hurt, and she didn't like how much that upset her. With a sigh, she made her way down to him.

When she reached him, Grace knelt beside him and looked over his body. There were burns everywhere. She bit her lip and gently turned him onto his back. There was no ignoring the fact he was completely naked. His entire torso was littered with wounds. Yet he was still breathing.

She blew out a relieved breath and found herself shaking with a mixture of happiness and concern. Now, she had to get him up and back inside the cave. Since he was so much taller than her, not to mention he outweighed her with all those muscles, she wasn't sure how she was going to accomplish that feat.

Grace glanced at the other guy and picked up a rock to bash him on the head. She got to her feet and cautiously walked to him.

She pushed him with her foot, but he didn't move. Grace gave him a harder push, turning him onto his back. She dropped the rock as she gagged at seeing a gaping wound in his chest where his heart had been.

Whoever the man was, he wasn't going to be bothering Arian anymore.

Grace hurried back to Arian. His eyelids cracked open as she leaned over him. Grace gave him a nod. "We're going to get you back in the cave."

"Scared," he murmured brokenly.

At first Grace thought he was saying he was afraid. Then she realized he was speaking of her. There he was on the side of a mountain injured terribly, and he was worried about her.

Grace could only stare at him, wondering if men like him really existed. Most people would be concerned about themselves, but not Arian. His thought was of her.

Then it hit her. She had seen him as a dragon. Was she afraid? Yes, in many ways. But how could she be scared now as Arian lay wounded?

She licked her lips and met his gaze. "Yes. But my father didn't raise me to leave someone who is hurt. So, I'm going to get you back into that mountain. Then I'm leaving."

The last part had been more for herself than him. She really should leave, but how could she after all she just witnessed? Remaining meant her life was in danger, as was obvious by the battle she had seen.

Then there were Arian's wounds. Someone would need to help him. It was the least she could do since he let her stay and write in his mountain.

Dragons.

Yep, the man she was looking down at was a dragon. Why wasn't she more scared? Most people would've been running for their lives. But there was something about Arian that calmed her. She trusted him.

Arian gave a slight nod in response to her words.

Grace winced as she looked down at him. "This is going to hurt."

At that, Arian rolled back to his side slowly and began to sit up. She was there to lend a hand and keep him steady. He was tall and muscular, and Grace wasn't sure how she was going to get him on his feet, much less up the slope to the cave. But she was going to try.

Once he was on his feet, he only put a small fraction of his weight on her. Grace draped his arm over her shoulder and wrapped an arm around him.

The climb up to the cave was as strenuous as she imagined it would be. Both of them were soon covered in sweat. Grace tried to take more of his weight to help him.

It seemed to take an eternity to reach the entrance. Arian breathed a sigh when they stepped inside the cave.

"Water," he said, motioning with his other hand to the body of water.

Grace walked him to the fire and helped him down. He stretched out on his right side with his eyes closed and didn't utter another word.

She hurried to get a bottle of water from the basket and brought it to him. While she held it to his lips, Arian drank the entire bottle, never opening his eyes.

Grace put the cap on the bottle and sat on her haunches as Arian appeared to slip into unconsciousness. Her mind urged her to leave, but she hesitated. What if there were more of those black and silver haired men about?

She would rather take her chances here with Arian than encounter one of those men. Then she also wanted to see if Arian would speak of what had transpired.

Besides, if she saw something she wasn't supposed to, running would do her no good. Arian and any others like him would find her soon enough. So Grace remained.

She got another bottle of water from the basket and one of the napkins. After she soaked the cloth napkin, she began to clean Arian's wounds.

Her eyes drifted freely over his magnificent body, from his wide shoulders, contoured stomach muscles, and trim waist. Then lower to his narrow hips and his flaccid cock.

She bit her lip at seeing so much of him when he was unconscious, but with a body like his, it should be showed off.

"Oh my," she whispered as she drew in a stuttering breath.

There wasn't a part on Arian that wasn't absolute perfection. And she wanted to touch every inch of him.

Chapter Six

Grace was wondering how to get Arian out of the mountain and to a hospital when she noticed his wounds didn't look quite as bad as before.

As she watched, she saw his injuries begin to heal. The burns disappeared and his skin knitted back together without a trace of any damage.

"Oh, shit," she murmured.

"Doona be afraid," Arian said.

Her gaze jerked to his face where his champagne eyes were open and watching her. "Yeah, a bit late for that."

"I didna mean for you to see any of that. I thought you'd still be asleep."

Grace shrugged and fiddled with the now useless napkin. "But I did witness it."

"Aye. You did." Arian pushed himself up into a sitting position.

She pointed to his now healed wounds. "What was that out there?"

He eyed her for several long, silent moments. Then he said, "Magic."

"Magic," she repeated. Well, she did see a dragon. Would it be too far of a stretch to accept magic as a weapon?

"You didna leave. Why?" Arian asked.

Grace looked at his chest again as she imagined him as a dragon. A huge dragon with the most beautiful turquoise scales that reminded her of the waters off the Bahamas.

The fear she had first felt was melting away. Now, it was desire—hot and insistent—that filled her. "I told you. I couldn't leave you out there wounded. Although, if I'd known you could heal, then I would've."

When she looked up at his face, Arian was grinning. As if her words amused him. He was supposed to be hurt by her words, or at the very least annoyed. Not amused.

She raised a brow. "You find that funny?"

"I like that you speak your mind."

"I probably shouldn't do that," she said as she got to her feet and moved away from him. "You might get angry and turn back into a dragon."

His smile vanished in an instant. He rose to his feet in one fluid motion, with his long black hair falling about his shoulders and his champagne eyes focused on her. "I doona harm the innocent, Grace. That man out there," he said, pointing through the entrance, "wasna a human. He was a Dark Fae, and he was looking for this cave."

Grace held up her hand to stop him. "Wait. Just...wait. I'm sorry, but I don't think I can handle all of this. It's too bizarre. And why are you telling me? Shouldn't you be demanding that I keep my mouth shut at what I've seen?"

"Would anyone believe you?"

She gawked at him, wondering why she hadn't thought of that possibility herself. "I don't believe what I saw."

"Aye, you do."

So she did. He didn't need to rub it in. Couldn't he see she was trying to pull herself together? Grace tossed the napkin in the basket and shrugged. "So what if I do?"

"You want to know more."

Damn. Was she an open book for him to read? This was not going her way at all, especially since she couldn't figure out what he was thinking no matter how hard she tried.

"So you'll tell me all I want to know and let me leave?"

"Aye."

At this, Grace laughed. "That's not how this works."

"And you've been in this situation before?" he asked with a quirked brow.

Grace opened her mouth, then promptly shut it. After a moment, she said, "Of course not. I'm merely going off what I've read normally happens."

"And that would be what, lass?"

"You threaten to kill me if I tell anyone."

Arian smiled, and it was devastating. Like a sucker punch right in her gut. Grace couldn't look away from his mouth and the sexy way his lips tilted.

"If it would make you feel better, then I could threaten you," he said with a half-smile that was by far too seductive.

She knew he was making fun of her, but Grace couldn't get upset. She sounded like a lunatic, which was insane since she wasn't the one who had been in the form of a dragon recently.

"You may no' believe it, lass, but you're safe with me."

Grace scratched her nose. "With a dragon?"

"Aye."

"You were a dragon," she said. "A huge dragon with wings and fire and everything."

He gave a nod. "I ken exactly what I am, lass. Have I hurt you in any way?"

"You know you haven't."

"And I willna. Unless you're here to harm us."

Grace couldn't stop the bubble of laughter that welled up. It escaped her lips. She looked at Arian, wondering about his sanity now. "You're a *dragon*. How could I possibly hurt you?"

"We have enemies. The Dark Fae are just one set. They want to out us to the world so that our existence would no longer be hidden from humans."

She wrapped her arms around her middle. "So there are more of you?"

"Aye."

"Many?"

"Enough."

"Oh." Shit. Grace lowered her gaze. There were dragons in Scotland.

And she had somehow walked into a cave where one had been. What were the odds that would happen?

He pivoted, causing her eyes to return to him. That's when she caught sight of the dragon tattoo on his left leg. It was done in an amazing black and red ink that she'd never seen before.

The tattoo began at his left hip, where the head of the dragon was looking up at him. The body ran down his thigh with the dragon's wings tucked and its claws looking as if they were sunk into Arian's skin. The dragon's tail dropped to his knee before curling around it.

The design was exquisite, but there was something about the placement that was incredibly sexy.

Grace had trouble breathing. No matter what her brain said, her body was attracted to Arian. It was partly because he was so gorgeous it hurt to look at him, but it was also because of the way he had held her so gently, how he spoke to her in that brogue that made her heart melt, and how he had struggled to help her up the mountain despite his own injuries.

He walked past her, and God help her, Grace turned and watched him, her gaze dropping to his amazing ass. She hastily turned back around when he grabbed his jeans at the entrance and put them on.

Grace drew in a deep breath. How was she expected to think after seeing something so mouthwatering as Arian's body? She had felt that warm skin. She knew how hard his muscles were, how powerful he felt—even injured.

Arian came to stand in front of her with his jeans now fastened. "Sit down with me, Grace. Let me explain since you've already seen who I really am."

When he turned and walked to the fire, she dropped her arms and followed. He was right. She wanted to know. She was insanely curious about him.

If she hadn't seen him with her own eyes, she wouldn't have believed he was a dragon. But she had seen. Up close and personal.

She sat on the opposite side of the fire from him. Grace watched as the flames danced between them, the firelight casting everything in a red-orange glow.

Their eyes met, and she waited for him to begin. Her heart was pounding slow and steady as a thread of exhilaration wound through her.

"We have lived on this realm since the beginning of time," Arian began in his deep, sexy voice. "For millions of years, the only beings on this earth were dragons. It wasn't airplanes that dominated the skies, but dragons."

Grace was immediately sucked into his story. She held her breath, waiting for him to continue.

"There were millions of us. From the smallest dragons, about the size of a cat, to the largest, like me. We were divided into factions based upon color, and there was every color imaginable. Each group was ruled by a king. The one of us with the most power and magic, immortal and lethal. Then there was one above a Dragon King—the King of Kings."

She was trying to imagine all the dragons in various sizes and colors upon the land instead of humans. Grace couldn't fathom it.

"Life was good," Arian continued. "I can still remember what it was like to look up and see dragons flying. Or to be in the sky and look down to see dragons dotting the ground. But those days are long gone."

"What happened?" Grace asked.

Arian looked away for a moment. Then he said, "One day mortals were here. Each Dragon King was suddenly changed into human form to communicate with them. We were then able to shift back and forth at will. We vowed to protect the humans."

Grace worried that the next part wasn't going to be so fun to hear. Especially by the way Arian's face tightened.

"We had peace. For a time. The mortals reproduced at an astonishing rate. Soon we had to move dragons out of areas they had always inhabited to make room for the humans. Even some of the Kings took mortal females to their beds. Some wanted those females as their mates, or wives, if you will."

She raised her brows. The best way to keep peace was an alliance, and what was a marriage but an alliance? It was the perfect solution, especially if there was love involved.

"One of the Kings, Ulrik, was about to take a female as his mate. Somehow Constantine, the King of Kings, discovered that Ulrik's woman was planning to betray him. She wanted to kill him. Little did she know she would never have been able to do it."

"Why?" Grace asked. "Was she weak?"

Arian smiled, but it was cold and hard. "The only one who can kill a Dragon King is another Dragon King. There isn't a weapon in any of the realms that can kill us."

Well, that certainly explained it. "Oh."

"Con sent Ulrik away, and all the Kings gathered together and hunted down the female. We killed her for her attempted betrayal."

"You killed her?" Grace asked in shock.

Arian nodded. "Ulrik brought her into his home. He clothed her, fed her, protected her, and loved her. Because to be taken as a mate to a Dragon King brings immortality to a human. So aye, Grace, we killed her. But Ulrik was angry at our actions when he found out. He wanted to be the one to end her life. In his grief and rage, Ulrik focused on those he felt responsible."

"Humans," Grace said.

"The mortals retaliated quickly and began to slaughter dragons left and right. There was no end in sight, and nothing any of us could do could stop Ulrik on his quest to rid this realm of humans."

Grace frowned at his words.

"Some of the Kings, myself included, joined Ulrik for a time. Con eventually brought all of us back together. All except for Ulrik. By this time, the mortals were intent on wiping out the dragons."

"But the Kings couldn't die by a human's hand," she said.

Arian nodded. "True. But they were killing dragons. We had no choice but to send all the dragons away. Then, once more the Kings gathered, except this time it wasn't to help Ulrik. It was to bind his magic and prevent him from shifting. We cursed him to walk this world for eternity in human form."

Grace grimaced. "Ouch."

"The war had to end. We hoped with Ulrik taken care of it would cease, but it didna. Even without dragons, the mortals hunted us."

"You could've wiped us out, right?"

Arian gave a single nod.

"Why didn't you?" she asked.

"We made a vow to protect the mortals. We take such promises seriously."

Grace shook her head, not understanding. "But you lost your dragons in the process. That's not right."

"It's what was decided. We returned to Dreagan and safeguarded it with magic to keep everyone off our land as we slept away centuries waiting for mortals to forget."

"Dreagan?" Why did she know that name? Then she realized it was the famous Scotch whisky.

Arian paused for a moment. "Dreagan is our home. It's the one place we can be our true selves. We hide here. Ulrik, however, has no' given up on his vengeance. He's teamed up with the Dark Fae, another old enemy, to expose us to the world."

She thought back to the questions Arian had asked her. "You thought I was working with Ulrik or the Dark Fae?"

"Aye. They've been known to use mortals to aid them."

"I'm not helping them," she said.

Arian's smile was slow. "Aye. I ken that, lass."

Chapter Seven

Arian tried several times to look away from Grace, but he was drawn back to her dark blue eyes again and again. The fear he had seen earlier wasn't gone completely. But it was tempered, calmed.

She sat casually, listening as he spoke. Her muscles weren't tense, and she was engaged in the story. Even asking him questions. He hadn't been sure how she would react, truth be told.

"How is Ulrik's attempting to show the world there are dragons helping him?" she asked.

Arian saw her gaze lower to his chest and her pulse quicken. His own body reacted viscerally. It was a primal, instinctive desire that flared hungrily through him. His cock hardened instantly, and it was everything he could do to remain on the opposite side of the fire from her.

He vaguely recalled that she had asked a question. Arian searched his mind and tried to get himself under control. "Ulrik wants to defeat Con and take over the Dragon Kings."

"Which means what for all of you?" Her navy eyes rose to his face.

"He could kill us."

Her brow furrowed deeply with concern. "Would he?"

"I doona know. It's a possibility. What I know he'll do is wipe the world of any human, and he'll begin by waking his Silvers and unleashing them."

Grace visibly swallowed. "Oh. Wait. What? There are dragons here? I thought you said they were sent away?"

"Four of his largest Silvers remained with him. We trapped them and keep them sleeping in one of the mountains."

"I see."

"It's no' just ourselves we're trying to save. It's your race as well."

Her gaze moved to the fire as she sat silent for a long moment. She took a deep breath and asked, "Why didn't Con kill him in the beginning, when Ulrik's magic was stripped?"

"Con and Ulrik were as close as brothers. They were opposite sides of the same coin. Con was steadfast and reserved while Ulrik was outgoing and a bit of a jokester. Despite their different personalities, they would've died for the other. Until Con became King of Kings."

Grace shifted, her head tilting to the side as she looked at him. "What happened?"

"That's between Con and Ulrik, but Con doesna talk about it. Or he didna when I was awake."

"Awake?" she repeated.

Arian briefly looked at his hands. "I've been sleeping in my mountain for six centuries."

"Your..." she began, her voice trailing off. Grace looked around the cavern before her gaze returned to him. "This is your mountain?"

"Aye. Each Dragon King has his own."

"I...wow."

He bit back a smile at her surprised reaction. "Many of us take to our mountains for long periods. Some get tired of hiding who we truly are, some have pasts they need to escape from for a while, and others must disappear from the world for a generation or so before reappearing."

"Which one are you?"

"A bit of all of them."

"Six hundred years is a long time though."

Arian lifted one shoulder in a shrug. "I had no intention of waking any time soon. The war with Ulrik and the Dark, however, changed that. Con had all the Kings who slept woken."

"Why were you going to remain asleep?"

"There was no reason for me to be awake. I know mortals have advanced considerably, but that doesna make our lives easier. In fact, it makes keeping our secret hidden even harder. Sleeping through the centuries makes things easier to deal with, like missing my dragons."

"I understand now."

He waited as she took it all in, digesting it bit by bit.

"Back to Con and Ulrik," Grace said. "Did no one think Ulrik wouldn't one day want revenge?"

Arian clasped his hands together as he rested his arms on his knees. "He was never supposed to unbind his magic."

"Um, what?" she asked with wide eyes.

"We bound his magic. Dragon magic is the strongest magic on the realm. No' even the Fae can beat dragon magic."

She nodded slowly, her face frozen in shock. "Yeah, ok. But you just said his magic was never meant to be unbound, which means that he somehow managed to do just that."

"Aye, lass, he did."

"And he says it so calmly," Grace mumbled to herself with a little shake of her head.

Arian found her completely fascinating. He was enthralled with every facet of emotion that crossed her face—and there were dozens. She hid nothing, whether on purpose or not, her emotions were there for all to see.

Grace dropped her head in her hands and blew out a loud breath. "You just said dragon magic was the strongest. What could possibly have beaten that?"

"An anomaly in the form of a Druid."

At this, her head snapped up. "Did you just say a Druid?"

"Aye."

She scratched her eyebrow and looked at the ground. "If there are dragons and Fae, why not Druids?"

Arian was hiding another smile.

When she returned her eyes to him, she shot him a flat look. "You can stop laughing, because yes, I'm wigging out to the Nth degree here."

"You doona appear to be...wigging out," he said, trying the word.

She moved her hands in a vertical circle in front of her chest. "It's all inside."

Arian's smile grew. If she only knew the truth about how he was falling for her. His smile faded as he thought of her leaving, because she would—eventually. He wasn't ready for that yet.

Without a doubt he had been alone in his mountain for a considerable time, and his body yearned to be near Grace again. He longed to touch her skin and feel her lips moving beneath his.

His emotions were so volatile that lightning streaked across the sky, followed immediately by a clap of thunder before the skies opened up once more.

Grace let out a shriek and jumped to her feet, getting as far from the entrance as she could. She faced the rain, backing up as she did.

Arian got to his feet and moved in her path. He used his body to block her from running into a boulder. As soon as he laid his arms on her shoulders, he felt her shaking.

"It's just a storm, lass," he whispered near her ear.

"It's never just a storm."

There was something in her words that caught his attention. Not too much the words themselves, but the depth of emotion in them.

Arian turned her to face him and looked into her deep blue eyes. He needed to take her mind off the storm, because he had no intention of stopping it. As long as it rained she would remain with him.

Once he had his fill of listening to her sweet voice and watching her feelings cross her face, then he would stop the rain.

"Bad things happen in weather like this," she said.

Arian smoothed back her hair from her face. "No' all bad, surely."

"My mother left us in a storm. My father died while a storm howled. I walked into a mountain with a Dragon King who is in the middle of a war with Dark Fae."

He was going to reassure her that all would be fine, but he couldn't find the words. The knowledge that so much pain was associated with storms made him question using his power to keep her with him.

But perhaps there was a way he could help her.

"Rain waters the earth, giving life to plants and flowers that are food for animals. The thunder and lightning are displays of the beauty and fierceness of nature," he said, hoping he could get her to accept his words and erase her fear.

Her body was pressed so enticingly against him. The feel of her breasts made his cock twitch. He looked down at her lips to find them parted slightly. Damn, but he wanted to taste them.

He couldn't breathe. The weight of the need, of the overwhelming desire felt like he was being pulled under. As if he were drowning, and Grace was the only thing that could save him.

The beat of her pulse at her throat was erratic and her chest rose and fell rapidly.

She felt it too.

Arian lifted his gaze to her face to find her eyes heavy-lidded as she watched him. He searched those amazing eyes of hers as he sank, tumbled into the navy depths.

He leaned his head forward until their breaths mingled. Her fingers tightened on his arms. Arian could stand it no more. He put his lips against hers.

She sucked in a quick breath. Arian moved his lips over hers, learning the feel of them before he touched his tongue to them, tracing them.

Grace leaned against him. He wound his arms around her, holding her firmly. A low moan filled him when her tongue touched his.

He was about to explode. Inside was a hunger he could never remember having before, a yearning to claim her right then that shocked and excited him.

The kiss deepened, their tongues intertwining seductively, sensually. Her lips were soft, her taste decadent. He slid a hand into her hair and held her head as their passion grew rapidly.

The soft kiss was turning as untamed as the craving inside him, and the more she responded, the more the flames grew. Her soft moans were driving him wild, but it was the way she breathed that made him burn.

He kissed down the side of her jaw, listening to her short breaths filling the air as she clung to him. His tongue licked her neck, and he felt a shiver race through her.

Then her hands grabbed his face and brought him back up so they could kiss once more. He couldn't get enough of her kisses or the way her hands roamed over his shoulders, arms, and chest.

He had to have her. There was no going back for him now, not after having her kisses.

Not after tasting her desire.

He lifted his head and looked down at her swollen lips. They were still parted, still wet from their kisses.

"Don't you dare stop," she said and rose up on her toes.

Arian felt a nudge in his mind. He could hear Con's voice, but he didn't open the link. Nothing was going to come between him and Grace right now. There would be time enough later to hear what Con had to say.

Grace's finger dipped in the waist of his jeans, and Arian groaned. He jerked when her hand cupped his arousal on the outside of his jeans and gave him a squeeze.

He continued to kiss her as his hand lifted the hem of her sweater and undershirt to feel her skin. He caressed upward until he cupped her breast and massaged the mound.

It was Grace who broke off the kiss this time. She moaned loudly when his finger circled her nipple, causing it to harden. It took but a second to unhook the bra at her back and shove it aside so his palm could feel her breast.

When he held it once more, he tweaked the nipple, causing her to give a cry of pleasure. Their gazes were locked together, their desire palpable.

Arian teased her nipple, enjoying how desire darkened her gaze even more. It was Grace who grabbed her sweater and shirt and pulled them over her head. Her bra followed a moment later.

Now they stood toe-to-toe, hip-to-hip. Arian put his free hand on her neck and nudged her head to the side with his thumb. Then he kissed her neck below her ear, licking and sucking the sensitive area. Her moans spurred him on, urging him to continue.

All the while she unfastened his jeans and spread the opening so she could find his cock.

Arian hissed in a breath when her fingers touched the head of his arousal. Then she began to touch him, tempting and teasing him until he was breathing as heavily as she.

He was rough as he unfastened her jeans and shoved them down her hips. Then he lifted her in his arms and laid her atop her sweater before the fire. With one jerk, he had her boot off. The second followed a heartbeat later. And then her jeans followed. He hesitated when he spotted the red lace panties that he found unbelievably sensual.

After running his fingers along the lace, he removed them so that she was fully bared to him.

Arian was kneeling beside her, looking at Grace's beautiful body, from her pink-tipped breasts to her waist and flared hips, down to her sex. He blinked as he saw she was completely shaven.

"Fuck," he murmured before he leaned down for another kiss.

Chapter Eight

Grace's stomach clutched, her breathing came faster. She didn't know what it was about Arian that made her burn, made her...yearn.

From the moment he'd spoken with that amazing accent, she'd been taken with him. His conversation had by turns irritated and intrigued her, pushing her to believe the impossible after witnessing him in his true form. With his astute thinking and sharp mind, he was more than a match for her intelligently. Seeing that glorious body and to-die-for face only made her crave him more.

Then he had kissed her.

And what a kiss!

It was a kiss like none other. There was fire and a hunger that was both savage as well as tender.

At first.

Then the fire had come. The kiss had charred her, searing her from the inside out. Each touch of his tongue, each time those lips of his moved over hers, had been the most incredible feeling in the world.

Until he lightly bit her bottom lip.

Grace had clutched him as she squeezed her legs together from the intense desire that made her sex throb.

She'd needed to touch him. His skin was warm and the sinew firm beneath her palm. But it hadn't been enough. She wanted to feel *him*.

His thick arousal was pressed against her stomach. It had taken her forever before she got his pants undone, and then she was touching him. She could feel his member pulse in her hand as she stroked him.

Her attention was soon divided when he teased her nipple. All Grace knew was that she wanted him inside her. Now! She burned for him as she had never burned for another.

Then she was on her back, naked. And his voice, husky with emotion and desire murmured, "Fuck."

She had never liked words like that during sex, but from Arian it made her heart race and her stomach flip with excitement. And need.

Grace couldn't find any words, which was a first for her. The feelings of desire, pleasure, and longing swarmed her, but she didn't feel like she was drowning.

No, she felt just the opposite. Like she was just now living.

She swallowed, watching as Arian stood and roughly yanked off his jeans. Grace eyed his tattoo again. She couldn't wait to touch it, but first, she wanted Arian.

He put his hands on either side of her face and leaned over her, kissing her. It wasn't the fiery kisses of earlier. These were more sedate, languid, but still just as sensual and erotic.

She loved the way he could stir her with just a simple kiss. It brought chills to her skin.

He stretched out atop her, his large body covering hers as she opened her legs. Instinctively, her legs wrapped around him, holding him as close as her arms now did.

A moan rumbled in his chest, and Grace held him tighter. What was it about Arian that made her respond so passionately? There was a wildness about her in his arms, and it had never been there before.

She was eager, madly impatient to have him deep inside her. To feel him moving within her.

A sigh escaped when he bent and placed his lips around a nipple. He sucked hard before laving the turgid peak with his tongue until she was writhing beneath him.

But he didn't stop there. He moved to her other breast and teased that nipple just as mercilessly. Grace's body fairly hummed with desire that coiled tighter and tighter.

Arian scooted down her body, kissing his way as he went. He paused at the scar on her right side where she'd had her appendix removed fifteen years earlier. Then he continued downward until his warm breath fanned her sex.

Grace stared at the stalactites above her without seeing them. She held her breath while he kissed the inside of each thigh softly, slowly.

Then he gently licked her sex. Grace's mouth opened at the

wondrous feeling that spread through her. It was quickly replaced by a bright blaze of desire when Arian flicked his tongue over her clit.

The breath rushed from her lungs as her mouth opened on a silent cry of pleasure. He teased, he licked, he laved. Taking her higher and higher each time.

Her back arched from the intense pleasure. He held her hips firmly, refusing to let her escape his tongue. But she had no interest in going anywhere. Not when he was touching her so amazingly.

Grace was floating, allowing the bliss to sink through her. Then Arian's finger touched her sex, stroking just under his tongue.

Before she could even register that, his finger pushed inside her. Grace moaned when he began to move his finger in and out, twisting it as he did.

It was just a moment later before he added the second finger. Grace tried to breathe between the waves of pleasure, but it was too much. She could feel her body hurtling toward the climax and there was nothing she could do about it.

When the orgasm came, it swept her away completely. It was so intense, so powerful that she was helpless to do anything but feel.

It was as if she were falling endlessly through a pleasure-filled void led by Arian. Instead of panicking, Grace didn't fight any of it.

As the climax began to fade, Arian crawled back up to her. Grace pushed at his shoulders and rolled him onto his back as she kneeled beside him. She ran her hands over his chest and leaned over, breathing and kissing on his skin.

She moved closer and closer to his arousal, but each time she got near, she would go another direction.

He was moaning as he watched her, his champagne gaze focused on her face. Grace looked up and met his eyes. The desire she saw there caused her heart to miss a beat.

She stopped with her mouth breaths from his cock. It had been six centuries since he felt a woman or pleasure. Then, still holding his gaze, she took him in hand and let her lips slide over his head.

His fingers dug into her thigh. "Fuck, Grace. That feels so damn good."

Spurred on by his words, she began to move her hand and mouth, taking him deeper. She cupped his ball sac and massaged them with her free hand.

She was enjoying herself, but all too soon he had her on her back once more. Arian held her arms above her head with his. She looked down at their bodies.

Logic intruded through her desire-filled brain. Protection. She needed protection. "Condom," she said, hoping he had one. It wasn't as if she carried one in her laptop.

His brow furrowed. "I'm immortal, lass. I doona carry disease, nor do I pass it on."

"Uh, huh." That was great news. "I don't want to get pregnant."

He leaned down to kiss her nose. "Mortals can no' carry the seed of a dragon."

Oh. Well that was something she didn't expect.

Then all thought fled as he moved his thick cock to the entrance of her sex.

"Do you want me?" he asked.

Grace glanced up at him and nodded.

"Say it, Grace. I have to hear you say it."

"I want you. I want you inside me," she said breathlessly, unable to take her eyes off his arousal.

He shifted his hips forward until the head of him brushed her. Grace sucked in a breath and raised her hips for more.

"Look at me," he demanded.

Grace dropped her head down and looked into his face. He was the most beautiful thing she had ever seen. Even if he was a dragon. Or maybe because of it.

With their gazes locked, she gasped as he entered her. Little by little, he filled her, stretching her as he did.

"So damn wet," he murmured. "And tight."

She wanted to say something, but once more words deserted her.

With one last thrust, he was fully inside her. Since he was still holding her arms, she raised her legs and wrapped them around his waist. She smiled at him when she began to move her hips.

"Minx," he whispered with a grin.

Then he began to move, and all smiles vanished. His thrusts were slow and long, filling her deep. The tempo began to increase steadily.

He released her hands and leaned over her to give himself more leverage. Sweat slicked their bodies as he plunged hard and fast.

His long hair fell over his shoulders, tickling her, but she didn't care. She met his thrusts with her own, silently urging him on with her movement and her cries of pleasure.

To her surprise, she felt a second climax coming. She looked up to see him watching their bodies as they came together.

Grace cried out as the second orgasm seized her. It was even stronger than the first, taking her breath with it.

"I can feel your walls pulsing," Arian said. "Can't. Hold. Back."

She held him as they climaxed together. The strength of it carried them high, as if they were flying.

Grace had no idea how long she lay entwined with Arian. She opened her eyes to see him leaning on his elbow staring down at her.

He touched her cheek gently. She couldn't tell what emotion was on his face, nor did she try. She simply allowed the moment to happen.

Arian pulled out of her and rolled them so that he held her against his chest. She closed her eyes, content where she was. Only then did she hear the rain. The thunder and lightning had stopped, but the storm was far from over.

Chapter Nine

Arian was content to just lay with Grace in his arms. Not only had her body felt good, but it felt *right* to have her next to him now.

He knew she wasn't asleep. She tensed every time the distant sound of thunder reached her. He could end her discomfort with a mere thought, but halting the rain would allow her to leave.

And he wasn't ready for that yet. It was selfish for him to keep making her deal with her fear, but he couldn't let her go. Arian was happy. Actually happy. The last time had been before he sent his dragons away.

How could he even think of losing Grace now?

Arian looked down at the top of her blonde head. He wondered what she was thinking. There was no doubt she enjoyed their lovemaking. Her cries of ecstasy, and the fact she had two orgasms, told him he had pleasured her well.

That should make him feel good about the situation. Instead, he wondered if she wanted to leave. He also worried that she couldn't handle his world.

Arian's thoughts halted immediately.

Why would he care if she couldn't deal with magic and immortality and shape shifting? Grace was beautiful, intelligent, and extremely gifted in her writing, but that didn't make her more to him.

He tried to imagine walking her to her car and seeing her drive away.

And it made him want to bellow in fury.

No. He didn't want her to leave.

Ever.

Arian closed his eyes. How the hell had he gotten into this situation? He realized as soon as that thought entered his head that there was no answer. It could be a myriad of things that allowed Grace to sink deep in his soul.

Whatever the cause, she was there. And he was going to hold onto her. It didn't matter what Con or any of the other Kings had to say about it.

"You're quiet," Grace said.

Arian found himself smiling. He noticed that he had been lightly rubbing her back the entire time. "So are you, lass."

"I'm thinking."

"About?" he urged.

She snuggled closer to him. "Don't laugh."

"I would never," he responded solemnly because he had a feeling whatever she was about to say was about them.

Grace flattened her palm on his chest. "I've not been writing it correctly."

"Writing what, exactly?"

"Passion. I forgot what it was," she whispered. "I went off what I saw in movies or read, but I haven't...experienced...it in many years."

He didn't like thinking about other men being with her, but they were in the past. Where they would remain. "Were they no' good lovers?"

"They were all right, but without passion, it all feels...empty."

Arian tightened his arm around her before he rolled her onto her back so he could look into her face. "I'll be happy to show you several times a day."

Her smile was infectious. "You're up for that job?"

He looked between their bodies to his cock that was already hard again. "Oh, aye."

Her smile softened as she put her hand on his cheek. "I just met you, and yet it feels as if I've known you forever."

"Is that wrong?"

"No. It's just...scary."

Arian didn't want her to be scared of the storms or the feelings developing between them. "How, lass?"

"I feel there's a connection between us. I've felt it from the moment

I saw you. I don't instantly sleep with people I first meet, and yet I was drawn to you. I couldn't stop it, and I didn't want to."

"What we did is natural. There's nothing to be ashamed of."

"I'm not ashamed," she said as she ran her hand down his neck to his shoulder. "All I can think of is doing it again."

Arian returned her grin. "It's our connection that frightens you, aye?"

"Yes. There isn't the normal anxiety I feel around men I'm attracted to. With others there was nervousness and uncertainty, which can make relationships difficult to form. But with you, I'm comfortable. Except when I saw you in dragon form. Then I was scared out of my mind."

She laughed, but Arian heard the truth in her words. "Are you still afraid?"

"Of you?" she asked, eyebrows raised. "No."

Arian once more felt Con push against his head, shouting Arian's name. He opened the link long enough to tell Con, "*I need a moment.*"

"There are more of us," Arian told her.

Grace swallowed. "Yeah. Those I might be a tad nervous around."

"I willna let them harm you."

Her navy eyes softened. "They're your brethren. You would do that?"

"Without question."

Grace closed her eyes for a second before she said, "Where have you been all my life?"

"Waiting on you to find me, lass."

She laughed and pulled him down as she wrapped her arms around him. They remained like that for several moments. Arian knew he couldn't hold Con off forever, but he also suspected that Con would want to interrogate Grace himself. With the war, they were all on edge.

Though Arian was assured Grace was innocent, Con would have to be certain as well.

Arian rose up to look at her. How he wanted to stay right here in this moment, but it was fading no matter how desperately he clung to it.

"Tell me about you," she pleaded.

Since he wasn't ready to answer Con, he touched the tip of her nose with his finger. "What do you want to know?"

"Everything. We all have pasts. I want to know yours."

"Aye, I do have one." He leaned on one elbow and traced figures on her stomach. "I was the only child of my parents."

"Dragons."

"Dragons," he said with a nod. "I'm glad they were no' alive to see the war with the mortals."

"Did they know you were a Dragon King?"

Arian smiled, recalling that special day. "That they did. They were so proud."

"Do dragons mate for life?"

"That we do."

Grace stretched her arms over her head, causing her breasts to poke in the air as she smiled. "I like that. I like that a lot."

Arian ran a hand down her side, wanting to be inside her again. His gaze followed his hand down to her hip where she had the leg closest to him out straight and the other bent, leaning against him.

"Did you have a mate?"

Arian nuzzled her neck. "Nay. After what happened with Ulrik's woman, Con cast a spell over us no' to feel anything for humans. We couldna fall in love again."

"Oh," she said softly, hurt in her gaze.

That pleased him immensely. "All that changed when Ulrik's magic was returned. It erased Con's spell, and Kings have been mating with mortals for several years now."

"So you didn't have anyone?"

Arian paused briefly. "I had lovers, aye. I didna get attached to them because of the spell. My duty and honor to Dreagan and the other Kings always came first."

"So you chose honor over love?"

"I was never in love," he reminded her. "But aye, when Con gave me orders, I did them."

Grace regarded him solemnly. "You left those women, didn't you?"

"I did."

"Why did you change sides from Ulrik to Con in the war?"

He groaned as Grace brought his attention from her body back to the conversation. Arian focused on her face, glad she had changed the conversation. "I understood why Ulrik was out to kill mortals, but I didna see a good outcome. We made a vow to protect them."

"But they tried to kill you."

Arian shrugged. "We had been around millions of years, Grace. We were the adults and the humans like children. We shouldna have reacted so harshly."

"You didn't. Ulrik did."

Arian thought about how he might feel if Grace betrayed him. For the first time he began to understand a fraction of what Ulrik went through. "Whether the blame is on the female who was going to betray Ulrik, on us for killing her, or Ulrik for starting the war, the fact is, everything changed for both races."

"What does all this mean for me? I know you asked me many questions when I first arrived. Will there be more?"

"Aye, lass, there will be. Con will want to meet you."

Her eyes widened a fraction. "Oh. Well...that...I didn't expect that."

Arian kissed her, loving the feel of her lips and the way she responded to him. "It'll be fine, lass. Answer him as you answered me."

He heard Con's voice in his head again. Arian could no longer hold him off. He lay back and pulled Grace against him.

"*Aye?*" Arian asked as he opened the mental link.

Con's voice was as frigid as a Scottish winter when he asked, "*Should I even begin to guess what you've been doing?*"

"*I'd rather you no'. As I'm sure Ryder has already informed you, everything Grace told me has checked out.*"

"*That means nothing. You know that. Ulrik likes to get humans to work for him. We doona suspect them, or so he believes. I also want to know how she saw your entrance.*"

Arian knew exactly what Con was getting at. "*You want me to bring her to the manor.*"

"*I do. Immediately. We need to know for sure if she's working for Ulrik.*"

"*You might ought to know that she saw me in true form.*"

There was a long pause. "*Did you intentionally allow her to see you?*"

"*Of course no'.*" It was Arian's turn to get angry. "*She was supposed to have been sleeping when I went out for a flight. I spotted more Dark on my mountain, and I took care of them. Sometime during that, she woke and saw the fight.*"

"*She'll need her memories wiped by Guy.*"

Arian didn't bother to argue against it now. He would once they were at the manor and Grace had proven she wasn't with Ulrik.

"*I'll have one of the Kings drive her car around to the distillery. Bring her through the mountains.*"

"*You would show her that?*"

Con chuckled. "*Aye. Watch her reaction, Arian. I want every detail.*"

The link was terminated. Arian remained where he was, still unwilling to leave the serenity they had found in his mountain. Grace was all smiles and kisses now, but as soon as they left everything would change.

But Arian couldn't wait. The sooner Con realized Grace was no spy, the sooner Arian could spend more alone time with her.

"How about some hot food?"

She shifted her head so that she was looking up at him. "We have to leave, don't we?"

Arian nodded. "Aye, lass. We do."

"I figured we might. This couldn't last forever."

"We'll return."

Grace's smile was sad as she sat up and reached for her clothes. "Sure we will."

Arian caught her hands and made her look at him. "We will. It's going to be fine."

"It's not that I don't believe you, but I'm a realist. You're in the middle of a war. Things like this never go easily."

"I'll be beside you the entire time."

She gave him a smile that didn't quite reach her eyes. "Let's get this over with."

He watched as she rose and began to dress. After a moment, Arian stood and tugged on his jeans. He gathered her laptop and jacket then waited after he left her keys next to the picnic basket.

As soon as she faced him, Arian bent and took one of the logs from the fire. He used his magic to put out the fire and gave a nod to Grace. "Stay close. There are some tricky spots."

She fell in step behind him as they walked to the back of the cavern. Arian took the tunnel to the far left. He had to duck to enter, but Grace passed through effortlessly.

He glanced over his shoulder at her often, but she stayed close to him. The tunnel was narrow at this part with nothing to see. Up ahead was a different story altogether.

"We're going deeper," Grace whispered.

Arian threw her a smile. "That we are. We'll go down and then back up eventually."

"How far do we need to walk?"

"A ways, lass."

"How far is that, exactly?"

He chuckled at her irritated tone. "We're going in almost a straight line to the manor. It'll take us a third of the time than if you were walking over the mountains."

"That means we're going to be walking for a while," she said with a grin.

It had been a long time since Arian had walked these tunnels, but it was something none of the Kings forgot.

"These aren't here naturally," Grace said.

"We made them after we took to our mountains. We had to stay hidden from the humans completely. So we dug tunnels to connect all the mountains."

"But these are only big enough for a human."

Arian paused and looked at her. "The ones we'll be walking are, but there are a few large enough for dragons."

"This is all real, isn't it?"

"I'm afraid so."

She shook her head in disbelief. "I'm still in shock over it, I think. I was ready to walk on water to run away when I saw the dragon. I knew it was you, because I saw you change, but I still have a difficult time grasping it all."

"Few mortals know of us, Grace. Several Kings have taken females as mates, so you'll most likely see them at the manor."

Her lips parted. "I'm glad the Kings have forgiven us."

"Many have, aye. There are still some who may never forgive humans for the war."

"I can't imagine a world with dragons."

He started walking again, holding the torch up so that it shed enough light so she could see where she was stepping. They walked for a long time in silence.

With every step toward the manor, Arian began to worry. Con had never liked the idea of the Kings taking the humans as mates. Yet nine Dragon Kings had done just that.

"How does Con feel about the mates?" Grace asked.

Arian raised a brow as he glanced back at her. "Do you read minds, lass?"

She laughed, the sound bouncing off the stones. "No. Why?"

"I was just thinking that nine of us have taken mates. Though one of them is a Fae."

"Obviously Con is fine with it then."

Arian flattened his lips as he considered her words. "That's no' entirely true. He's been known to step in and try to dissuade pairings."

"Has he succeeded?"

"Nay."

There was a quick intake of breath as she tripped and reached for him. Arian righted her and gave her a nod to see if she was all right.

Grace shoved her hair out of her face and dropped her hands to her side. "Does he want the Kings to be lonely and miserable for however long you live?"

"Eternity. And aye, he does if it means we're no' betrayed."

Chapter Ten

Eternity. That's what he said.

Grace could hardly fathom such a length of time. "You don't die?"

"The only way for a Dragon King to die is—"

"By another Dragon King," she said over him with a nod, remembering his earlier words.

The light from the torch flickered off his face, singeing the edges of shadows with red and orange. It gave Arian's champagne eyes an amber glow.

In such a few short hours her life had changed. Before her stood not just a man, but an immortal dragon. And a King at that.

He made love to her as if he knew everything she wanted and needed. Though he might believe that she wasn't a spy, the others wouldn't be so easily convinced.

Of that, Grace was certain.

"Come, lass," Arian said and took her hand.

She followed him another dozen steps before the tunnel melted away and she found herself standing in a cavern. It was half the size of Arian's, but even with the little light from the torch she could see the glint of gemstones.

Out of the corner of her eye, she saw Arian watching her before he whispered a few words. Suddenly a ball of light flared above them, rising higher and higher while its light grew brighter and brighter.

Grace gasped when she saw not just the gemstones embedded in the rock, but dozens of drawings and etched stone of dragons. Every inch of stone was marked in some way.

"We took turns sleeping those years we waited until the humans forgot us. Those that remained awake dug tunnels. And passed the time with these."

"Wow," she whispered.

There were no words to describe the magnificence of what she was seeing. It wasn't just beautiful and amazing, it was wonderful and inconceivable.

And it was a little sad as well.

To know that Arian and the others were trapped below ground for centuries was just wrong. This planet had been theirs until her kind arrived. Humans were like a plague. They destroyed everything and everyone. Just like what they had done to the dragons.

"What is it?" he asked when she lowered her gaze.

Grace turned her head to him. "I saw you in your true form. You were scary, yes, but also incredible. Seeing all of this makes me depressed knowing my race was responsible for keeping you from the skies where you belong."

His arm wound around her waist as he pulled her against him. He kissed her softly, gently before he rubbed his nose against hers.

She laid her head on his chest and looked at the cavern again. It was pretty, but to not see the sun? No wonder so many Kings hated her kind.

"Doona fash yourself about it, lass," Arian whispered.

She straightened from him. Without a word, he dropped his arm and continued walking. Grace followed as they skirted one part of the cavern. She could see several different tunnels that could be taken.

Arian walked past four before he took the fifth one. They encountered no one, but Grace had the feeling that others were there. Other Dragon Kings, that is.

She didn't see them. It was just a feeling. Or perhaps it was the weight of what the humans had done to the dragons that pressed upon her as she saw more and more drawings and carvings.

Grace touched one dragon drawing she glimpsed from the torchlight. It was no bigger than her hand, and for some reason it struck her right in the heart. Such a tiny dragon after seeing so many huge ones on the walls.

Arian glanced back at her often, but there were no more words between them. The closer they came to the manor, the more worried she became. And the tenser he became.

She was tired. Some parts of the tunnels were relatively smooth and easy to walk. Other parts were like hiking in a minefield with all the boulders and dips and valleys in the rocks.

Thankfully, those treacherous places were few and far between and were only short distances. But her exhaustion and anxiety were taking a toll on her.

Tunnel after tunnel they walked. She lost count of the caverns they either passed through or she saw a glimpse of through an opening. Arian never hesitated in the direction he was taking her.

Grace realized that she was putting a lot of trust in him to be taking her so deep in the earth. He could be a serial killer.

The thought made her giggle. He was a dragon, not a serial killer. And though she knew his secret, she didn't really know him.

Why then was it so easy to be around him and so comfortable to talk to him? She usually only felt that way with people she had known for years. Certainly it had never happened with someone she barely knew a handful of hours.

Her father had often warned her that her greatest gift—and biggest weakness—was that she trusted so certainly.

How many times had that trust been burned? And yet each time she found herself trusting again. It was a weakness, a flaw, and yet it was who she was.

It put her in positions to be deceived, mislead, and lied to on various occasions.

However, it had never put her in a position to lose her life, and that's exactly what she felt was at stake here. Arian hadn't said anything, but he didn't need to. It was in the way he held his jaw.

Just when she was about to collapse and ask for a break, she saw a light ahead of them. Arian said another word, and the torch extinguished instantly.

"We're here," he said.

Grace looked ahead in the tunnel. "I need to know the truth. If I don't answer Con the way he wants, will he kill me?"

Arian's face softened as he smiled and cupped her cheek for a quick, hard kiss. "Nay, lass."

"He won't just let me go though."

"We have our secret to maintain."

"Well, he can't keep me here," she said, thinking of the next viable option.

Arian sighed and dropped his arms to his side. "There's another way."

"What way?" she pressed.

He paused before he said, "One of the other Kings has the ability to wipe memories."

She blinked, unsure if she had heard him correctly. "I'm sorry. Did you just say wipe my memories? So you'd leave me wandering the streets without knowing who I am?"

"Nay, no' at all. Guy will only wipe away anything you've seen or learned while here."

"Meaning you."

Arian gave a single nod.

Grace wasn't about to give up her time with Arian. It was special, and she had the right to hold on to those memories.

Just as the Kings had a right to protect themselves.

"I understand," Grace said. "I don't like it, because I don't want to forget you, but it's better than being killed. Still, I don't want my memories wiped. I'm going to do my best convincing that I'm telling the truth."

"I know you will, lass."

How she wished she could see his face better as he stared at her, but the shadows had taken over once more. Grace was relieved when he slid his fingers in hers and took her hand.

Together, they walked toward the light as the tunnel opened wider. When she saw the door that seemed to go into the house, she knew the time had arrived for her to face the King of Kings, Con.

Grace took a deep breath and slowly released it. Arian opened the door and she walked into the manor from what appeared to be nothing more than a wall. A hidden doorway. As if she would expect anything less after all she had learned.

"It's going to be all right," Arian whispered as he closed the door behind them.

She followed him through the house where there were once more dragons everywhere. Some were obvious, like the iron dragons that seemed to come from right out of the wall while holding a light in a claw, to others, not so discernable in paintings.

They passed near the kitchen where she could hear female voices and laughter, followed by a deep baritone. Arian didn't so much as look in the direction as he led her onward.

When they came to the stairs, Grace looked outside to see that the rain had finally stopped as morning dawned. At least that was one thing she wouldn't have to deal with.

She placed her hand on the banister, only noticing then that the wood was a dragon as well. A glance back at the newel post showed the head of the dragon, with every detail from its scales to its teeth painstakingly carved.

Grace ran her hands through her hair, trying to straighten what she could. She probably smelled, and she knew she looked awful. She'd much rather meet Con showered and dressed properly, but that wasn't going to happen.

Arian reached the landing and proceeded down the corridor. Grace wondered where the next set of stairs led to, and she had the insane urge to find out right then.

Anything to delay seeing Con. She felt like a kid being sent to the principles office in elementary.

As if sensing her nervousness, Arian smiled at her. Grace attempted to return it, but her nerves were too wound up to manage more than a slight tilt of her mouth.

All too soon Arian stopped next to a closed door. He gave her an encouraging nod, then opened the door. There was no time at all for Grace to collect herself before she was standing before a tall man with penetrating black eyes that were as cold and desolate as a desert.

They were in stark contrast to his bright blond hair that was cut short on the sides and longer on top. Con wore a pair of black dress slacks and a burgundy dress shirt that was unbuttoned at the neck and his sleeves rolled up to his elbows.

Arian and Con clasped forearms like something out of the middle ages. Whatever was passed between them was done silently, because no words were spoken aloud, but Grace was sure something had been said.

Then Con's midnight gaze was on her again. He looked her up and down without any emotion on his face. Grace was beginning to think he was a robot to not show any kind of reaction—good or bad.

"Grace Clark," Con said in a deep, clear voice. "Thank you for coming to see me."

"I didn't have much of a choice."

Arian spoke up then, "But she came freely, Con."

Con looked from her to Arian and back to her. "Freely?"

"Arian told me you needed convincing." Grace shrugged. "That's what I'm here to do. I also know that if what I say isn't satisfactory that my memories will be wiped."

"It seems Arian told you a great deal," Con said, showing his first signs of annoyance with the tone of his voice.

Grace lifted her chin. "Shall we proceed? I have a book that has to be written."

Con turned to the side and motioned to the chairs before his desk with his arm. Grace walked past him and took the one on the right. Only once she was seated did Con move to stand behind his desk.

He stared out the window for a time. Grace tried not to fidget in her chair, but the silence was cruel and unusual punishment when she knew Con wanted answers.

She drummed her fingers on the arm of the leather chair and looked around the room, seeing a medium-sized chest with a rounded lid off to one side. It looked ancient. There was a sideboard where a decanter filled with a gold liquid and several crystal glasses sat.

It was the pinging on the window that drew her attention. Grace looked outside to see the sky had darkened, as if night had changed its mind about allowing the day to break.

Lightning flashed in the distance, forking over the mountain. Grace barely noticed the dots of white on the mountain until the sheep began to run in a group to shelter.

Another storm. This was the last thing she needed. She gripped the arm of the chair and tried desperately not to show how she was affected.

Then Con turned and pinned her with a look.

And she knew it was too late.

Chapter Eleven

Arian didn't look around the manor at all the changes that had taken place while he had been sleeping. With Con visiting each of the sleeping Kings and updating them on the goings on in the world and how humans had advanced, Arian was up to date on technology.

No, Arian's attention was on Grace. She gripped the arms of the chairs tightly, making her knuckles white in the process. She was nervous, and she had every right to be.

Constantine hadn't changed in six centuries, not that Arian expected him to. If anything, Con had gotten colder, more aloof. He was completely detached from the world.

"Keep the storm going," Con said in his head.

After everything he and Grace had shared with each other, Arian felt ashamed for what he was doing. Yet, he told himself that the sooner Con got his answers, the sooner Grace wouldn't need to endure her fear anymore.

Arian turned away from the window and grabbed the shirt folded on the edge of Con's desk. It was plain and white, but Arian didn't really see it. His focus was on Grace.

She convinced him of her innocence. All she needed to do was persuade Con as well. The problem was that to Con, everyone was an enemy.

Nothing Arian had tried to argue on his and Grace's journey to the manor swayed Con. Con's argument was that Arian hadn't been involved in the shite that had been happening.

In other words, Arian was soft.

Which infuriated him. Arian might not have been fighting these past months, but he fought plenty enough before. He was one of the last to find sleep after the Fae Wars. Not to mention that it took a lot to convince him to change his mind once he made a decision.

Con, however, had used a low blow. He suggested that Arian had been influenced because of Grace's body.

"Tell me what brought you to Dreagan, Grace," Con asked.

Arian could hear the weather getting out of control. That was his doing because he couldn't get a handle on his anger. He drew in a deep breath and slowly released it, the storm abating some.

Grace swallowed and looked Con in the eye. "As I told Arian, I checked into the B&B where I'm staying. From there I went driving, looking for a place that was quiet and where I could be alone. I drove deeper into the mountains. I had no idea where I was going. I drove until I reached the mountain and could go no further."

"There was no road there."

She gave a slight nod. "It's true the road was more of tracks in the grass. I was curious and wanted to see where it would take me."

"How long did you drive before you came to Dreagan?"

"I didn't know it was Dreagan," she said in an unsteady voice, her gaze going to the window as the rain pinged against the glass. "As for how long I drove, I've no idea. I wasn't timing myself."

Con walked around the desk and came to the front of it, leaning his hands and hips back against it. "You don't know what time you left the B&B?"

"It was around ten or so," Grace said with a shrug.

Arian wanted to go to her and stand beside her. To give her strength and to show Con that Arian was going to protect her. It might come to that, but Arian sincerely hoped it didn't. Surely Con would come around to see what Arian already had—that it was merely fate that brought Grace to him.

"When did you arrive at Arian's mountain?" Con asked.

"I don't know. An hour or an hour and a half later. I didn't really look at my watch. I had no one waiting for me or anyone to answer to. Why would I keep track of time?"

Con looked down at her boots. "You dressed for hiking."

Grace laughed wryly as she straightened her leg so that it was horizontal as she regarded her shoes. "These aren't hiking boots. They're old tennis shoes that wouldn't do me a bit of good," she said, her voice growing louder in her anger. "Would you like to comment on my raincoat? Do you think I can make it rain at will?"

"Oh, I'm no' worried about you having that ability," Con said and glanced at Arian.

Arian fisted his hands. He might have told Grace much about his race, but he hadn't told her about his ability to control the weather. He rarely used the ability, preferring to let the realm take care of itself.

But there were instances, like earlier when he needed to keep her in his mountain, that it came in handy.

Grace's gaze swung to him. Arian gave her a small nod. If she saw it, she gave no response as she returned her eyes to Con.

"That's right," Grace said, jerking when more thunder boomed. "I'm just a human. I'm mortal. I've no magic or the ability to shift into a dragon. I am who I say I am—a novelist. I'm sure with the money Dreagan brings in that you have the ability to do a search on me. Do it. Find out all that you need. Hell, go to a bookstore and find my book."

Con raised a blond brow. "Perhaps you made up everything that we'll find. We've friends in MI5, Ms. Clark. We know what lengths someone will go to in order to hide who they are."

"Not me," she insisted. Her voice pitched higher in frustration. "I'm a freaking nobody! I came here to try and find my muse again. My writing groove left me. It said *adios* and vanished months ago. If I don't turn that book in three weeks from now, I lose my contract. My book is set in Scotland. That's why I'm here."

Arian knew Ryder had already given Con all there was to know about Grace. Ryder, in his infinite skill, had dug up every single thing there was to know about Grace from the day she was born until now.

Even Ryder had cleared her. So what was Con up to?

"And how did you find the cave entrance?"

Grace gaped at him. "This again? I saw it. With my eyes. Why is that so odd?"

"Because it was cloaked with dragon magic," Arian answered.

Grace's eyes went wide. "I don't have an answer then. I saw it."

Could Grace have been meant to find his mountain and him? Arian was beginning to think so. Because there was no other explanation. The barrier around Dreagan hadn't kept her out, and she'd seen his cave entrance—both of which had dragon magic.

"I doona believe in accidents, Ms. Clark," Con said in a soft voice. "I doona believe you just happened to find Arian's mountain."

Arian inwardly cringed. That voice had lulled plenty of others before Grace. It belied the anger and awareness within Con, as well as his purpose.

Grace blew out a breath, her face going white as lightning speared from the sky to the ground. "Well, we'll have to agree to disagree then, because I believe life is nothing more than a multitude of accidents and coincidences."

"You make light of your situation?"

"Absolutely not," Grace stated. "I know how serious this is. I also know that Arian believes me. Why isn't that enough for you?"

"Because I believe Arian is being ruled by his cock."

Grace gasped the same instant Arian narrowed his gaze on Con.

"Trust me," Con said in Arian's mind.

Arian had always trusted Con, but to have him talk in such a way to Grace was nearly impossible to bear. Slowly, he released the tension in his body.

Grace was shaking her head. "You think so little of Arian then? That's...well, that's just sad."

"Sad?"

"Yes," she said firmly. "I ran into that mountain to escape the storm. A few hours later, I saw Arian in dragon form fighting the Fae. If I'm to believe everything Arian has told me, all of you are in the middle of a war. You should trust your people."

There was a push against Arian's mind and then Con said, *"Ramp up the storm. I need lightning."*

Arian hesitated. Never before had he wavered in doing as Con ordered, but now he was having serious doubts. Grace was shaking, her face was white, and she was sweating from her fear. To put her through more was too much. Arian couldn't take it.

"Arian," Con urged. *"Trust me."*

Trust. That's what Grace had put in him. Arian had vowed he would protect her from everyone and everything. He wasn't doing that now. She was innocent. Con would see that. He had to.

With a deep breath, Arian did as Con requested. The first flash of lightning made Grace jump in her chair and squeeze her eyes closed.

It killed Arian to purposefully scare her in such a manner, but if it could end the interrogation earlier, then he would make it up to her later and explain his power.

If she let him.

"Trust is something I doona give lightly," Con said as his head leaned to the side while he studied Grace. "What about you?"

Grace pulled her eyes away from the window to look at Con. Her head nodded jerkily. "Yeah. I trust easily. Don't bother to tell me it's wrong. Plenty of others have."

"So you trust Arian?" Con pressed.

Grace jumped when more lightning flashed, followed by thunder that sounded all around them. She yelped, then said, "Yep. I do."

Arian exchanged a look with Con. Would this be all Con needed?

"More lightning and thunder," Con demanded.

"She's afraid of it. Can you no' see that?"

"Of course I can."

Arian should've known he wouldn't get an explanation, but then again, it went unsaid. Everything Con did was to ensure their secrecy.

It hurt Arian physically to put Grace in such fear, but he had no choice. If Con didna get what he needed then Grace would have her memories wiped. She would wake up at the B&B never knowing how deeply she touched his soul when they kissed or how he ached to be buried inside her once more.

She would never know how much he wanted to be with her.

Con was in favor of wiping her memories regardless of if she was working with Ulrik or not, but Arian wasn't going to let that happen.

He needed Grace. It was because he needed her that he did as Con asked once more.

After this was all over, Grace might leave and want nothing to do with him. Arian wasn't about to give up on her that easily though. If something was worth having, it was worth fighting for.

That meant against his own kind as well as Grace.

There was something special between him and Grace. It was something profound, something that never came near Arian before.

Until Grace.

He watched her complexion pale with each bolt of lightning. Her body tensed as the thunder rumbled loudly around them. Each moment that passed made her curl into herself.

And it was slowly killing him.

"Get on with it, Con!"

Con cut him a look before he focused on Grace. "Who do you work for, Ms. Clark?"

"Myself," she answered without taking her eyes off the window.

"That's no' true. Who do you work for?"

She shrugged, slinking farther into the back of the chair. "My pub...publisher. I work for my publisher."

"You work for Ulrik, do you no'?" Con pressed.

"No." She let out a shriek when several rounds of lightning struck in quick succession.

The more anxious Grace became, the angrier Arian got. And the more extreme the weather became until he couldn't get it under control.

Arian desperately tried to rein the weather in, but it was nearly impossible as he listened to Con push Grace again and again to see if she would change her answer.

Every trembling "no" that fell from her lips only infuriated Arian more. She gripped the chair so tightly that he heard the wood crack.

"What are you doing at Dreagan?" Con demanded.

"I already told you!" Grace screamed as thunder made the manor shake.

Arian looked to Con to find Con watching him. Even with that icy stare, Arian knew Con's thoughts. Con recognized that somehow in the few hours Arian was with Grace, that something transpired between them. Something more than just sex.

And Con wasn't happy.

"*Finish it,*" Arian insisted.

Con's gaze slid to Grace. "Do you work for Ulrik?"

"No! For the twentieth time, no!" Grace screamed.

But there was something in her voice that sent warning bells off in Arian's head. He looked to her then. Grace's gaze moved from Con to the window to Arian and back to Con several times.

Her face crumpled as she rose and hurried around the chair to put distance between them. She shook her head as she stared at Arian with navy eyes that were filled with sadness—and a hint of anger.

"Grace," Arian said and took a step toward her.

She held up a hand to halt him. "Stop," she ordered and blinked past the tears that began to fall. She then pointed to the window. "That's you. You've been doing this. All this time here and in the mountain. You used my fear against me. How could you?" she yelled.

"I ordered him to do it," Con said.

Grace ignored Con as she stared at Arian, wincing as another bolt of lightning struck. "I thought you believed me."

"I do," Arian said.

Grace sniffed and turned to Con then. "Do whatever you're going to do to me, but I'm done here."

"Grace," Arian began.

But Con stopped him. "Give her some time, Arian."

Arian waited for Grace to look his way. After several tense moments, he realized that wasn't going to happen. It took numerous tries to halt the storm. When he had, he left the room with a sick feeling in the pit of his stomach growing with every step he took away from her.

Chapter Twelve

The tears dried quickly as the numbness took hold. It was worse than the day her mother left. Even worse than when her father died.

She had trusted, as she always did, and it had once more come back to bite her. She should've known Arian was too good to be true.

A man like him who was too gorgeous to even look at, immortal, and a Dragon King didn't choose someone like her. It had always been about their secrecy.

If only he had been honest with her from the beginning. But why would he? They were in the middle of a war. Not even that thinking could stop the hurt from spreading.

"Can I get you anything?" Con asked.

She closed her eyes. How could she have forgotten she wasn't alone? Grace blew out a breath and shook her head as she looked out the window. She wrapped her arms around herself while the clouds dissipated and the sun came out. "No, thank you."

"I did what had to be done. I'll no' apologize for that."

"Then don't." She'd had enough of Con. He and everyone else needed to go step on a Lego and fall in a hole.

Out of the corner of her eye, she saw Con push away from the desk and stand. "Remain here, Ms. Clark. I'll return in a moment."

As soon as the door closed behind him, Grace turned and stuck her tongue out. It was immature, but it was either that or cry some more.

Grace couldn't believe Arian had manipulated her fear in such a way.

Then again, she could. If her very way of life was threatened, there was no telling what she would do. She recalled vividly the extremes she went to in order to save her father from his heart failure.

On one hand, she didn't blame Arian, but on the other, she did. They'd shared something personal and beautiful together, and she felt manipulated.

Grace glanced at the door. She was supposed to wait for Con. If she were braver, she would take her chances and make a run for it.

She looked at the door again, her heart kicking up a notch at the thought of making a run for it. But that's exactly what she was going to do.

A look around Con's office didn't show her keys or her laptop. But that wasn't going to stop her. She didn't care if she had to steal a car, she was getting out of there.

Grace didn't hesitate. She hurried to the door and quietly turned the knob. When the door cracked open, she looked into the corridor. No one was in sight. She opened the door wider and poked her head out, looking both directions.

There was a small voice in the back of her mind that reminded her something terrible could happen if she got caught. But she wasn't going to get caught. She had been used enough. It was time to leave Dreagan.

Grace slid into the hallway and quickly closed the door behind her. She remained against the wall and half-ran, half-walked to the stairs.

She paused when she reached the steps because once she was on them, anyone could see her. Grace took in a steadying breath and then held her head high as she descended the stairs.

At the bottom she had a moment's fear since she didn't know where to go. Then she decided it didn't matter. She turned left and found herself walking down a wide corridor with windows on one side letting in tons of light. On the opposite wall were paintings and tapestries of dragons of numerous sizes and colors. She came to a door and peeked inside to find it was a library.

Grace pivoted and retraced her steps since it didn't look as if she was going to find a way out in the direction she had been going.

She found the stairs again easily enough. This time she went to the right. After a bit of maneuvering around open doorways with others inside what appeared to be a parlor, Grace found the front door.

As soon as she was outside, she breathed a sigh of relief. She faced forward and saw her rental car parked right in front. Grace ran to the vehicle and got inside. There she found her keys in the ignition, her purse and laptop on the seat beside her. Her hands were shaking as she started the engine and threw the car in reverse.

It wasn't until she was driving away that she felt something heavy in her chest, as if her heart were breaking in two. All that she had shared with Arian was gone. She thought he was different than other men, but she had been wrong. He was a man who cared more about Dreagan and the Dragon Kings than he did about her.

Grace pressed the accelerator. The car gained speed as she turned onto the main road. She didn't have a clue where she was going. All that mattered was that she left the Dragon Kings behind.

Something fell on her cheek. Grace swiped at her face, infuriated to find that it was a tear.

"I'm not going to cry for Arian," she told herself. "He's not worth it."

The sad part was that he was *definitely* worth it. He was the type of guy she had been writing in her novels for years. The type of guy that she only thought existed in her mind. Not once did she ever believe she would find him.

But she had found him. That's what hurt so much. He had been in her arms, real and so wonderful she hadn't been able to stop touching him.

Kissing him had been mind-blowing. So much so she hadn't ever wanted to stop.

He had been kind and gentle, tender and sweet. All while having an air of danger and mystery that made her so hot for him.

His immortality made her a bit wary, but how could she be afraid of a Dragon King who made love to her like he was worshipping her?

She hadn't expected anything of Arian. Well, that wasn't true. She knew what she wanted from him, and she had hoped he wanted more from her as well. Knowing what he was and the war he was part of would've made things difficult, but it didn't deter her.

Arian hadn't just touched her physically. He had changed her. She always thought she had an open mind, but discovering his secret had forced her to challenge herself and her thinking. She had accepted who he was, as well as his story. Grace yearned to help him any way she could.

The few hours with him had altered her mind, her body, and her heart. Now she looked at the world entirely different because she knew there was magic and dragons, Fae, and Druids walking around.

How wonderful she had felt being with him.

Then Arian had to go and ruin it by using her fear against her.

Grace shifted gears and found the signs leading back to Inverness.

* * * *

Warrick stood with Con at the front of the manor, watching Grace Clark drive away. "Are you sure this was the right thing?"

"She wasna lying. She's no' working with Ulrik," Con said.

Warrick raised a brow as he cut his eyes to Con. "That's no' what I'm talking about, and you know it."

"Is it no' enough that one more King has chosen a mate? Arian just woke. He needs to be focused on the war."

Warrick crossed his arms over his chest and faced Con. "You saw how Arian reacted. I believe Grace could be his mate."

"Perhaps."

"Perhaps?" Warrick repeated. "Just what lengths will you go to in order to keep a King from his mate?"

Con turned his black eyes to him. "If I think there could be another repeat of what happed with Ulrik—anything and everything."

"Grace isna that type of woman."

"You doona know her."

"Neither do you," Warrick pointed out. "The only one who knows her at all is Arian. And I tell you, he's no' going to be happy when he learns what's happened."

"And what has happened?" came a voice behind Warrick.

Warrick turned and spotted Arian standing in the middle of the doorway. Warrick hooked his thumb toward Con and said, "Ask him."

Arian met Con's gaze. "Where is Grace? I went to your office, but no one was there."

"She's gone," Con said.

Warrick watched Arian closely. A muscle ticced in his temple and his nostrils flared as he attempted to keep calm. It was just a few days earlier Warrick had felt those same emotions. Just as he imagined, Arian was thinking of throttling Con.

"Gone?" Arian asked tightly.

Con nodded. "You were right. She was telling the truth about who she is."

"And you allowed her to leave knowing our secret?" Arian asked in disbelief.

Con glanced at Warrick and said, "Does that sound like something I would do?"

Warrick watched Con walk from the room. He gave a shake of his head and sat down in one of the chairs. Con had said he would go to any lengths. He had just proven it.

"I didna see Guy," Arian said. "I wanted to tell Grace farewell."

Warrick wasn't going to sit there and allow Arian to think Grace had her memories wiped. And surely Con knew that. Which made Warrick wonder just what the hell Con was up to.

"Her memories were no' wiped," Warrick said.

Arian's head jerked around, his long black hair falling over the white shirt. "What?"

"Con didna have Guy see Grace. He left her alone in his office, and just as he expected, she made a run for it. We stood here and watched her leave."

Arian ran a hand down his face. "I'm going to kill him."

"Ulrik may very well beat you to the punch, my friend."

"Why?" Arian asked helplessly. "Why would Con make me believe Grace was out of reach?"

Warrick shrugged and got to his feet. "Because he's an arse. Because he doesna want us to be happy. Because he doesna want to be the only one without a mate. Because he can. Take your pick."

"Why did he no' wipe her memories?"

Warrick shrugged. "That I can no' answer."

"Fuck, this is messed up."

"I could tell you all the ways that he's made it difficult for some Kings to have their mates, but that would take too much time. You need to go after Grace."

Arian looked out the window. "Con knew you would tell me the truth. I wish he would've done it."

"No' in the bastard's DNA."

"I hurt her, War."

Warrick nodded as he recalled doing the same to Darcy. "Aye, I know that feeling well. If you think there's something there, then go to her and do or say whatever needs to be done or said to get her back."

"Fight for her."

"Aye. Fight."

"That I can do."

Warrick smiled as he watched Arian stalk from the room. He looked upward to the room where Darcy was still asleep in their bed after hours of lovemaking.

He was supposed to be getting them something to eat. He made his way to the kitchen and began to gather items as he thought of all the ways he still wanted to make love to his woman.

Warrick was walking up the stairs when Arian came running down in a pair of boots, his same jeans, and a leather jacket over his tee shirt.

"I doona have a vehicle," Arian said.

Warrick laughed and jerked his head toward the garage. "You've no' actually driven yet, either, but you'll get the hang of it. At least you willna kill a sheep as Kiril did. Take the top set of keys. It's to a white G-class Mercedes. You'll figure it out soon enough."

Arian went down a few steps then stopped again. "Where is she staying?"

"Ryder," they said in unison.

Arian was all smiles as he ran from the manor to the garage. Warrick hoped Con hadn't interfered too much to stop Arian from finding happiness.

Warrick was beginning to think that Con wanted everyone there to be miserable, which was shite, because they all suspected he had a lover.

The fact they had yet to find a woman he was with told Warrick it wasn't a mortal woman. Which left the Fae.

And no good would come of that.

Chapter Thirteen

Arian adjusted his grip on the steering wheel. He hadn't been awake in hundreds of years. The world had changed drastically from the last time he saw it, but he wasn't looking at the landscape. He was thinking of Grace and how badly things had gone wrong.

He flexed his toes, not yet used to the boots confining his feet. The clothes weren't much better, but then again, he had been in dragon form for a very long time. Nothing was going to feel right.

Except Grace's hands. They felt perfect against his skin.

Arian followed the directions from the female voice coming from the SAT NAV system. Driving wasn't that difficult. After he ran into a couple of things. The damage shouldn't be that bad.

He glanced up through the sunroof to the sky. A sky he wondered if dragons would ever be seen in again. He had a sick feeling they never would.

Pushing aside such morbid thoughts, Arian focused on what he would say to Grace. Everything that ran through his mind sounded awful.

Arian cringed when he heard the scrape of metal as he moved too far to the right and the SUV skidded against a wall of rocks as he drove across a bridge.

Seeing the damage done to the vehicle was the least of his worries. It was just a piece of metal. There was much more at stake—his heart.

His soul.

His future.

Arian didn't stop to wonder how he had come to feel so strongly about Grace in so short a time. All he knew was that he did.

That fear clutching at his heart was the same sensation he felt when he watched his dragons fly across the dragon bridge to another realm.

He had been helpless to do anything then. This time was different. This time he could set things right. And he was going to make sure he did.

No matter what he had to do or say, he wouldn't give up on Grace until she realized she was his. Because she had been. From the first moment she walked into his mountain, she had been his. Their fates had been sealed when they made love.

The B&B came into view. Arian slowed the SUV, his heart kicking up a notch when he spotted the car Grace had been driving.

She was still there. He hadn't realized how worried he was that she might have left until that moment.

Arian pulled over and stopped the vehicle. He shut off the engine. Then he rested his forehead against the steering wheel. He wasn't sure he knew what to do next.

It went without saying that he wanted Grace, but he had never gone after a woman before. If they wanted to be with him, great. If not, then he moved on.

With Grace, it was different. He had chased after her. He was even willing to get down on his knees and beg her forgiveness.

But where to start? A simple apology wasn't going to cut it.

Arian lifted his head and looked at the cottage across the street. Grace was inside, probably still upset. He recalled the fear in her pretty eyes and how they had welled with tears when she realized what he had done.

He'd hated himself at that moment. Though his actions had been to help safeguard his brethren, it had hurt Grace deeply. He'd promised to protect her, and instead he had done the opposite.

No, she hadn't been hurt physically. That didn't mean he hadn't harmed her emotionally and mentally.

Arian palmed the keys and got out of the vehicle. He closed the door behind him as he strode across the street. His hand shook when he knocked upon the bright blue wooden door.

The seconds that ticked by felt like eons as he waited for someone to come to the door. Finally, there was a creak in the floor when someone approached.

A moment later and the door opened to reveal a man in his early sixties with a solid white head of hair and gray eyes. He was beginning to hunch forward, but he stared at Arian with a clear gaze.

"Can I help you?" the man asked.

Arian gave a nod. "I'd like to speak to Grace Clark, please."

One thick, bushy white eyebrow rose. "Grace, aye? Stay here, lad, and let me see if she's in."

That was his way of telling Arian he was going to see if Grace would talk to him. Arian remained on the front step, trying not to fidget. He looked around the area, noting all the houses had taken the place of forests of trees.

Arian fiddled with the keys. He ran his hand through his hair. He kicked at the dirt on the path. He watched cars pass.

And all the while he thought of Grace.

He imagined running his hand along her face, of threading his fingers in her hair.

He thought of her smile, of the way her navy eyes lit from within when she gazed at him.

He remembered the touch of her hands on him, of the way she breathed when he was making love to her.

Then he recalled her fear, a fear he'd exploited. Her terror for storms went bone deep—so deep she might never get over it. He would try to show her the beauty of storms, but it would be asking a lot of her.

Arian knew then that even though it was his power, he was willing to never use it again if it meant he could be with Grace.

The door opened behind him.

Arian turned around, words already tumbling from his lips. But they fell silent as he looked not into the navy eyes of Grace but the old man.

"I'm sorry, lad, but she's no' available," the man said.

Arian looked above him to the windows of the second floor. Grace was up there. He could force his way in and make her talk to him, but what good would that do?

"I see." Arian hated the bitter taste of disappointment.

The old man's gray eyes were steady as he watched Arian. "Perhaps latter, lad," he offered.

"Perhaps. Thank you for your time," Arian said with a bow of his head. He then turned on his heel and walked back to the Mercedes.

Arian got back inside the vehicle and simply sat there. It wasn't a good sign that Grace wouldn't see him, but Arian wasn't about to give up. He would wait however long it took for her to talk to him.

He looked around the village. If the Dark could gain access to Dreagan, they could be there as well. Arian started the SUV and pulled onto the road. No Dark were going to get close to Grace.

* * * *

Grace's hands were shaking as she pulled her laptop on her legs and reclined against the iron headboard. Arian was there. To talk to her.

But she couldn't see him. Not now. Not after what he had done.

Everything bad in her life happened during a storm. For the first time, she had felt safe during the thunder and lightning as long as she was with Arian.

Then she learned he was controlling it, making the storm rage while Con interrogated her.

Grace didn't take an easy breath until she heard the SUV start up and drive away. She had seen Arian pull up, and much to her dismay, she had been ecstatic that he had come for her.

But she somehow found the courage to turn him away.

She opened a new document, the cursor blinking on the blank screen. She tabbed down and typed "Chapter One." Her fingers hovered over the keys for a moment, and then the words came out like a deluge.

She stopped seeing the words as she relived the scenes in her head. The smells, the sounds, the stillness of the water. The cool air, the heat from Arian's body.

His touch, his kisses.

The way he made her laugh and feel comforted.

The way he welcomed her into his world.

Hours later, she looked up to see that it was time for dinner. She surveyed the hundreds of pages she had written, stunned that it had all come so easily.

Words had never flown so effortlessly from her mind to her fingers, and she doubted she would ever again be able to write a story in so quick a time.

Then again, it was her story. She'd lived it, breathed it.

Survived it.

Grace set aside her laptop when there was a knock at her door. She rose and opened it to find Mr. McKean.

"Lass, you missed lunch and tea," he said, concern lining his eyes. "We didna want you going hungry."

At that he stepped aside, and one of the young girls helping at the B&B walked into her room with a tray in hand. The young girl came inside Grace's room and set the tray on the table.

"Eat," Mr. McKean urged Grace.

She blinked her tired eyes. "I will. Thank you for being so kind."

"That young man was brokenhearted that you didna see him, lass."

Grace lowered her gaze as she thought of Arian. She believed he might feel something for her, but more than likely he was concerned she might tell others his secret.

"He'll be fine," Grace said and smiled at Mr. McKean. "Thank you again for the food."

He returned her smile, and he and the girl walked away. Grace closed the door as her stomach rumbled. She sat at the small table and took a large bit of the shepherd's pie.

As she ate, she looked at her laptop. She was at the part of the story where Arian had driven away from the B&B. Grace knew what the future held for her, but this was where she could make it into whatever she wanted.

And since it was a romance story, the couple had to end up together. She might not get her own happily ever after, but her characters could.

Grace finished eating and returned to the bed. With the computer back in her lap, supported with a pillow underneath, she began typing once more.

It was easy for her to lose herself in the story. It was *her* story, after all. Her very own touch with having an HEA of her own. After the books she wrote and characters she lived through before she finally sold, she had never thought she would find anything close to what was in her books in real life.

And yet she had.

The part that hurt the worst was that it was over—before it had barely begun. It wasn't like she could delete parts and rewrite her story.

What happened, happened. There was no changing anything in her life like she could with the words on a page.

As she wrote the epilogue to the story where the characters—really it was her and Arian—remained together with a love that would last for eternity, she found herself crying.

Not just because the characters were in love and together, but because her heroine had been able to get over her fear of storms for the hero—something Grace wasn't sure she could ever do herself.

When the last period was typed, she saved the document, staring at the manuscript. She wasn't worried about her telling of the Dragon Kings, mostly because her books were fiction and no one would believe it anyway, but also because she changed all the names and locations just in case.

With a sigh, Grace closed the laptop.

For long moments she sat without moving, her gaze out the window. It had felt good to get her story out, but she was feeling a plethora of emotions.

Happiness at recalling her time with Arian.

Fear at reliving the storms.

Sorrow at having to say farewell to Arian.

And finally, gratification at being able to once more get her HEA— this time with her very own story, even if it wasn't in real life.

Grace blinked. Night had fallen without her even noticing. Was Arian up in the sky, flying? What did the moon look like reflected upon his turquoise scales?

Grace curled onto her side and closed her eyes as she imaged looking up and finding dragons soaring overhead. The fear she felt when she first saw Arian was gone, as if it had never been.

Now all she felt were possibilities for who the Dragon Kings were and what they could offer the world.

But she also felt desolation because she knew the Kings wouldn't be welcomed by all.

It was no wonder the Dragon Kings stayed hidden. And why they took their privacy so seriously. The world wasn't ready to know about them, magic, immortality, or the Dark Fae.

No amount of movies or TV shows or books could prepare a person for the real thing. The sheer size of Arian in dragon form alone was enough to make her feel as if her heart were going to burst from her chest.

With her eyes stinging from staring so long at the computer, Grace closed them. Her mind drifted once more to Arian and how he had so gently and possessively taken her into his arms and kissed her.

Another tear leaked from the corner of her eye. He was "The One." The one man who could've given her the great love she had always dreamed of. The one who was the other half to her soul.

To have held him so close only to lose him seemed too cruel for it to be real.

Chapter Fourteen

Arian paced Con's office. He had searched the village and didn't find a single Dark Fae or anyone who looked suspicious. Yet they had killed three more Dark who dared to try and enter Dreagan.

"You're making my head ache," Con said from his chair behind his desk.

Arian cut him a dark look. "You've never had a headache. You wouldna even know what one felt like."

"Oh, you'd be surprised."

Con's cryptic words halted Arian. He faced the King of Kings. "What are you no' telling me?"

"A lot, but that is the nature of my position." Con tossed his favorite moon pearl Montblanc fountain pen on the desk.

"You've always hidden things well, Con. Your anger, worry, anxiety. Even your fear."

"Fear?" Con asked with one blond brow raised.

Arian nodded and crossed his arms over his chest. "I want Grace as mine."

"You doona even know her."

"Are you my parent that I must convince?"

Con grew even more still. For long minutes he simply stared at Arian. "What I am is your king. What I do is for our continuation and survival."

"We'll always survive here," Arian argued. "Tell me, why did you no' wipe Grace's memories?"

"She left before I could."

Arian grunted. "You allowed her to leave. Admit it."

Con simply returned his stare.

"What are you up to?"

"I've told you."

"Do you have a lover, Con?"

"As if that's any of your concern."

"It is. As long as you interfere in my love life, I'll interfere in yours. Who is she, Con? Who is the woman you've been spending time with?"

"None of your goddamn business."

Arian blinked, taken aback by Con's words. It hadn't been an outburst as some who might have shouted those words. Instead, they were spoken in a cool tone. Entirely too controlled, which confirmed that whoever Con was seeing was important to him.

"One way or another I'm going to convince Grace to be mine." Arian dropped his arms to his sides. "I'll take the time to get to know her and for her to know me. But she'll be mine."

Con put his hands on the desk and slowly stood. He leaned on the desk and held Arian's gaze. "You're claiming her? Even though she may no' want you?"

"I am." Arian knew how she responded to his touch. She may not want him now, but he wouldn't give up until she remembered her initial reaction to him.

"All right," Con said and straightened. "I'll welcome her as I have the others. But I'll also warn you as I have the other Kings. I killed a human who betrayed one of you. I'll no' hesitate to do it again if need be."

"We were all right there with you, Con. You didna kill Ulrik's woman on your own."

"I was prepared to."

"Grace isna like that. She wouldna betray me."

"Ulrik thought the same of his woman. We may look like the mortals in this form, Arian, but we're no' them. And they are no' us. They doona think as we do."

Arian thought of Grace and her acceptance of him. "Perhaps no', but there are many other ways our two species are the same."

"We mate for life. Verra few of the humans even grasp that concept. They take marriage vows no' thinking forever. It's for the here and now. That's why so many commit adultery or leave the marriage when things get rough instead of working through it."

Arian put his hands on the back of the chair in front of Con. "You make it sound like we've no' made any mistakes. We've made plenty. We're no more perfect than the mortals."

"I could argue differently."

"Do you hate them?"

Con's black eyes became distant. "I doona know what you mean."

"I get the feeling you do, but then why do you defend them so fiercely? If you hated them, why no' allow Ulrik to rid the realm of them once and for all."

"We took an oath."

Arian shrugged one shoulder. "So you do despise them."

"I didna say that."

"You didna deny it, either."

Con adjusted the gold dragon-head cuff link at his wrist. "My feelings toward the mortals doona matter one way or the other. My first duty is to all of you and our way of life. Only after that do I consider the vow I took regarding the humans."

Arian looked past Con to the window. Night was still upon them. It was time to stretch his wings and look in on Grace.

After all, debating anything with Con was an exercise in futility.

* * * *

Grace's eyes snapped open. She sat up in the darkened room and glanced at her mobile. It had only been two hours since she finished the book.

She tried to lie back down and sleep once more, but her eyes wouldn't remain shut. She couldn't stop thinking about Arian. Or seeing the cavern in her mind's eye.

After another thirty minutes of tossing, Grace rose and took a shower, thinking that might help her relax and get back to sleep. But once out of the shower, she was more awake than before.

She dried off and put on clean clothes before she tugged on her hiking boots. Grace walked from her room with nothing but her mobile phone and a jacket.

As she strode from the back door of the B&B, Grace saw the rolling landscape before her. The moon didn't shed much light as it filtered through the clouds, but she had the flashlight on her mobile if she needed it.

The fresh air and a nice walk were just what she needed to empty her mind so she could find some peace. She strolled across the terrain. Occasionally she glanced upward, not that she expected to see anything. There were too many clouds for one, and for another, she didn't think any of the Kings would be this far from Dreagan.

Why then did she keep looking up? She tried to deny it, but the simple fact was she wanted to see a dragon. Correction. She wanted to see Arian.

She knew what he looked like with his wings spread as he soared through the sky. She knew how his turquoise scales glinted metallic in the sunlight. She knew the feel of the heat from the fire he breathed from his mouth.

Powerful. Dignified. Commanding. Mighty. Imposing. Noble.

They were all words she would readily use to describe Arian in both his dragon and human forms.

Grace was breathing heavily when she crested a hill that was a lot steeper than she had originally thought. She stood looking over the land even as a cold breeze blew past her.

She wrapped her arms around herself. Though she had traveled extensively all over Europe, she continued to set her stories in Scotland.

Her father used to laugh about it, telling her that there must be something in Scotland drawing her to the land. She used to roll her eyes at his teasing. Now she wondered if he hadn't been right.

Her father had believed in fate and destiny. Whereas Grace thought each person decided their own path with the choices they made.

Now she was beginning to believe that perhaps her father might have had it right all along. It felt as if she were supposed to have met Arian and experienced all that she had with him.

Destiny? Or choice?

There was a whoosh overhead. Grace looked up but saw nothing more than the clouds from before. She started walking forward down the hill.

Grace reached the bottom when she heard something above her. This time when she lifted her gaze she saw a dark shape begin to emerge from a cloud.

She gasped, mesmerized as Arian flew over her, circling back around by dipping one wing. The beat of his wings was so loud she wondered how no one else heard it.

Her gaze was riveted as he descended in one fluid motion with his wings outspread while he hovered over the ground before landing.

He tucked his wings against him and watched her with his black eyes.

Arian didn't move, and it took Grace a moment to realize he was waiting on her.

She licked her lips. What should she do? She was torn, wanting to go to him and wanting to run away. He had already come to see her once as a human. He had returned again. This time in his true form.

Grace walked to him one slow step at a time. Her heart was racing, but not because she was scared of him. Because she was frightened of how he made her feel.

She halted before him, looking up into his black eyes as he towered over her. Arian lowered his giant head, and Grace hesitantly stroked him.

A laugh escaped when she felt the warmth of his scales. They were hard beneath her hand, but not cold. It was so unexpected that she couldn't stop touching him.

He closed his eyes, a low rumble coming from deep within him. Grace rested her cheek against the side of his head. In all her wild imaginings, she never pictured herself caressing a dragon.

As odd as it seemed, it also felt as if she had been destined for it.

If only he hadn't used her fear against her.

Grace squeezed her eyes closed. Why did she have to be afraid of storms? Why couldn't she let go of the fear? If she could, she might have a future with Arian—because she had already forgiven him for what he did.

Because she loved him.

Arian blew out a breath and lifted his head. Grace stepped back as she watched him. For long seconds, he held her gaze, and then in a blink the dragon was gone. In its place was Arian, standing naked and proud before her.

Grace let her gaze run over him from his face to his feet and back up again, stopping to admire the dragon tat on his left leg.

It must be the trick of the light because she could've sworn it moved.

"Grace."

Her eyes lifted to his face, where she found him staring at her. His expression melted her heart instantly. He allowed her to see his sorrow, his anxiety, and his...love.

She took a step back when she realized what he was offering. Grace hadn't thought anyone could tell another of their love without words, but the proof stood before her now.

"I promised to protect you, and I didna," Arian said. "I let you down."

Grace didn't move, didn't so much as blink.

"I'm sorry. So verra sorry, lass." Arian looked at the ground for a moment and ran a hand through his hair. "Those words are so inadequate. I could say I did it for my brethren and Dreagan, but even that doesna sound right."

She looked at his wide shoulders. Those same shoulders where she had rested her head after they made love. She looked at his arms. The same arms that had held her so passionately and protectively.

"Say something, Grace. Please," he implored.

But she didn't know if she could. The words were stuck in her throat. Yes, she had felt wonderful with Arian, but she had also experienced her greatest fear while with him.

She loved him and already forgave him, but he chose loyalty over love. Would he do it again?

Arian let out a deep breath and gave a single nod. "You'll no' see anyone from Dreagan again. Of that, I vow. No one will take away your memories. Unless you want them gone."

Did she? It would be easier not having to remember Arian and his kisses, but was that really want she wanted? No!

"*Anything worth having is worth fighting for,*" her father used to say.

His second favorite quote was, "*Sometimes the most complicated things in life are the ones that end up bringing us the most satisfaction.*"

Arian and the Dragon Kings were definitely complications. And she wanted to be a part of that world. As alarming and thrilling and terrifying as it all was.

"I forgive you," she said as Arian turned to leave.

He jerked back to her. "Say it again. Please."

This time she had a difficult time not smiling. "I forgive you."

He was before her in a blink. Hesitantly, he hooked a finger with hers. "I'll never hurt you again, Grace. I put my loyalty to Con and Dreagan above my feelings for you. I did it because I wanted Con to believe you, so I thought that if he could get his information you'd never have to endure his question again. I'm sorry, lass."

Her eyes closed when he pulled her against his chest and wrapped his arms around her. Despite everything, in his arms was where she knew she belonged.

Chapter Fifteen

Arian held Grace tight. He let her go once. He wasn't going to do it again. Kissing the top of her head, he said, "I doona want to scare you, lass, but I've fallen for you."

There was a beat of silence. He felt her tense in his arms then. Arian knew he shouldn't have told her that yet. He was going to frighten her away just as he got her back.

"Arian," she whispered.

It was the thread of panic in her voice that alerted him. He jerked his head to where she was looking and saw the three Dark Fae approaching.

"*Dark Fae!*" Arian shouted through his mental link to the Kings.

He pushed Grace behind him as he looked around for more Dark.

Behind them another two came their way. It was their smirks that set Arian off. The Fae thought they had them cornered, but Arian wasn't about to let that happen.

"Do you trust me?" he asked Grace.

She clutched his arm and nodded her head quickly. "Yes, I trust you."

"Climb on my back. And hang on tight."

There was a strangled screech as he shifted as soon as she had her legs wrapped around him. Arian unfurled his wings, knocking two of the Dark back.

Another sent a blast of magic at him, hitting him squarely on the neck. Pain radiated through him as the magic sizzled along his scales.

If only he had thunder to mask a roar, but he wouldn't put Grace through that fear again. He would find another way to beat the Dark.

He opened his mouth and blasted the Dark with dragon fire. Grace had a death grip on him, but even so Arian was afraid to jump into the air and knock her off. It was her first ride, and he needed to be gentle.

But there was no such thing as gentle in battle.

A growl left him as he was hit with several more rounds of Dark magic. If he didn't get out of there soon, the Dark magic would make him shift back into a human.

Arian swiped his tail behind him. He severed a Dark in half, leaving only three more to fight.

"Make it rain!" Grace yelled.

Surely Arian heard her wrong. Grace would never tell him to make it rain.

Arian turned, using his tail to keep the Dark at a distance. His wings he used to deflect magic aimed at Grace. He took a couple of steps forward to take off when he was hit in the side with a volley of Dark magic.

"Arian! Do it!" Grace demanded. "Make it thunder."

His heart swelled at the trust she bestowed upon him. Despite her fear, she believed in him.

He let loose his magic. The clouds gathered quickly overhead, and a second later, lightning split the sky viciously again and again. Thunder rumbled so loudly that it masked Arian's roar as he was bombarded with Dark magic.

There was no mistaking the feel of Grace shaking as she clung to his neck. He had to get her away from the Dark and the storm. But the tempest was the only cover to get them out.

He took a huge chance dropping from the meager clouds to see Grace to begin with. Getting away without the storm would be impossible as the Dark tried to keep him there. Not to mention, the Dark didn't care who heard or saw them.

Arian prayed Grace held on. He jumped into the air, spreading his wings, and caught a current. With a quick turn, he dodged another round of magic. As he swung back around to deliver a blast of dragon fire, two dragons came up on either side of him.

He met the royal purple gaze of the gold dragon. Con. With a nod, Con tucked his wings and dove toward the ground. Arian looked on the other side of him to find Warrick. Lightning flashed around them, giving Arian a glimpse of War's jade scales before he joined Con in taking out the remaining Dark.

Arian contained the storm to where they were and quickly flew Grace out of it. He kept as low to the ground as he dared without being seen as he glided through the sky toward Dreagan.

Finally, Grace lifted her head from his neck and looked around. He heard her whispered, "Wow," which caused him to smile.

Though he reached Dreagan swiftly, he didn't land. Instead, he wanted to show Grace the other side of being a Dragon King.

He dipped lower, taking them in the valley between mountains. Arian felt his heart swell when he heard her laughter.

"Arian, this is amazing!" she yelled.

Her grip eased, but it didn't loosen altogether. Finally, after another thirty minutes, Arian turned and headed to his mountain.

He slowed, using his wings to hover him over the entrance. After he landed, he walked through his entrance to the cavern. Only then did he lower his neck so she could slide off him.

Arian used his magic to start a fire for light. Then he shifted and yanked her into his arms. He buried his head in her neck. "I'm so sorry I had to use the weather."

"It's all right."

"Nay. It's no'."

She leaned back to look at his face. "No, it really is. I knew I was safe with you. I knew you would control the weather so it couldn't hurt me. I should've realized that sooner. It was us in danger that made me face what I already knew."

"I'll never let anything hurt you, Grace. Ever," he vowed.

She glanced down at his chest. "Before the Dark arrived, you were saying something."

"It doesna matter. It can wait."

"Say it again," she urged.

He looked into her navy eyes and felt the steel band of anxiety ease from his chest. "I'm falling for you."

"Falling? Or fallen?"

"Fallen," he admitted. "I fell for you the minute you walked into this mountain. Does that frighten you?"

She gave a small nod. "It does."

Arian knew he shouldn't have told her his true feelings. Not yet anyway. She needed time to adjust.

"It does because this isn't suppose to happen," Grace said.

"What?"

"Love at first sight." She put her hands on his chest and smiled. "Everyone says it can't possibly happen, but I know that it does."

Arian's heart beat faster. "And? What do you think it means?"

"I'm not sure. All I know is that I like how I feel when I'm with you. I love how protective you are and that you aren't afraid to say you're sorry. I like how you touch me and kiss me. I like how you hold me, but more than anything, I like the possibilities that are before us."

"We're in the middle of a war," he warned.

She shrugged and ran her hands up his chest and over his shoulders to clasp around his neck. "Every couple has their own issues to get through."

He threw back his head and laughed. "I do love how you can make me laugh in such a way."

"I do, too. I also really like how you can make me hot for you with just a look."

Damn. Did she really just say that? Arian moaned, feeling his cock harden at the thought.

"That," she said breathlessly. "That's the look."

Arian kissed her hard, his arm holding her so tight he knew he was hurting her. But he couldn't loosen his hold. She was too precious to him.

He ended the kiss and simply held her, amazed that she had come into his life. "You found your muse again at Dreagan. Will you stay?"

"What of Con?"

Arian leaned back so he could look at her. "Con let you leave Dreagan. He watched you."

"What?" she asked, her brow furrowed.

"He believes you. I think he wanted to see how far I was willing to go and how much you could take."

She rolled her eyes. "I don't think I like him very much, but I know why he did what he did."

Arian smiled and tugged a lock of blonde hair. "Stay here with me, Grace. I want you as mine. Always."

"You don't know me."

"We'll take the time to get to know each other. But please stay. I need you."

She rose up on her tiptoes and placed her lips on his. "As if I could refuse such a request. I'm all yours, Arian."

"Damn, baby. That's just what I wanted to hear," he said as he claimed her lips for another fierce kiss and began to undress her.

Epilogue

Grace couldn't stop fiddling with her purse strap. The book was turned in to her publisher. Arian even liked the fact she used their story. But that's not why she was nervous.

Arian's hand came to rest atop hers gently. She looked at him and returned his smile as she gazed into his champagne eyes. "It's going to be fine," he assured her once again.

He had been saying that all morning. She believed it when they went to gather her things at the B&B with Mr. McKean smiling knowingly. She even believed as they drove away.

But the closer they came to Dreagan, the more worried she began.

"You trust me, right?" Arian asked.

"Of course."

"Then trust me when I say it's going to be all right."

She nodded. "My things are really being packed up in Paris?"

"The joys of being involved with such a large corporation. Things get done."

"That's money, Arian."

"Same difference," he replied with a grin.

She released a deep breath and sat back in the Mercedes. It was dented on both sides badly, though it made her smile to know that Arian had driven for the first time the day before to look for her.

His fingers threaded with hers when they turned onto the drive that wound through thick woods leading toward the manor. She caught a glimpse of red roofs and knew that was the distillery based on the descriptions Arian had told her.

He was going to take her on a tour later and show her everything. She was also going to meet everyone.

The manor came in sight then, the gray stones standing strong against the backdrop of the Highlands. The sky was bright blue without a cloud, and the sun was blinding. A perfect day.

Arian parked the SUV and turned off the ignition. He lifted her hand to his lips and kissed her fingers. "Ready?"

"Yes."

They got out of the car. Grace looked around at the mountains as she closed her door. Arian came up beside her and wrapped an arm around her. They stood together for several minutes.

"You're part of Dreagan now," Arian said as he looked at her. "Just as you're a part of me. That means our enemies could focus on you, but it also means everyone here will protect you."

"I don't know what to say."

"Say you'll be mine."

She smiled then. "I was yours from the moment I saw you."

"Then lets get your new life started."

They walked arm-in-arm to the front door. When they drew close, it opened and Con stood in the doorway. He gave a nod to Arian, and then bestowed a smile to Grace.

"It looks like another King has found his mate," Con said.

With that, they walked into the manor to a crowd of people waiting to meet her.

Through it all, Arian never left her side. His arm remained around her, offering comfort and support when she needed it.

Grace found herself looking at him often. And each time he was watching her. She couldn't believe she had gotten so lucky to find the man of her dreams.

It was only made better knowing he was a Dragon King.

Sign up for the 1001 Dark Nights Newsletter
and be entered to win a Tiffany Key necklace.

There's a contest every month!

Go to www.1001DarkNights.com to subscribe.

As a bonus, all subscribers will receive a free
1001 Dark Nights story

The First Night
by Lexi Blake & M.J. Rose

Turn the page for a full list of the
1001 Dark Nights fabulous novellas...

1001 DARK NIGHTS

WICKED WOLF by Carrie Ann Ryan
A Redwood Pack Novella

WHEN IRISH EYES ARE HAUNTING by Heather Graham
A Krewe of Hunters Novella

EASY WITH YOU by Kristen Proby
A With Me In Seattle Novella

MASTER OF FREEDOM by Cherise Sinclair
A Mountain Masters Novella

CARESS OF PLEASURE by Julie Kenner
A Dark Pleasures Novella

ADORED by Lexi Blake
A Masters and Mercenaries Novella

HADES by Larissa Ione
A Demonica Novella

RAVAGED by Elisabeth Naughton
An Eternal Guardians Novella

DREAM OF YOU by Jennifer L. Armentrout
A Wait For You Novella

STRIPPED DOWN by Lorelei James
A Blacktop Cowboys ® Novella

RAGE/KILLIAN by Alexandra Ivy/Laura Wright
Bayou Heat Novellas

DRAGON KING by Donna Grant
A Dark Kings Novella

PURE WICKED by Shayla Black
A Wicked Lovers Novella

HARD AS STEEL by Laura Kaye
A Hard Ink/Raven Riders Crossover

STROKE OF MIDNIGHT by Lara Adrian
A Midnight Breed Novella

ALL HALLOWS EVE by Heather Graham
A Krewe of Hunters Novella

KISS THE FLAME by Christopher Rice
A Desire Exchange Novella

DARING HER LOVE by Melissa Foster
A Bradens Novella

TEASED by Rebecca Zanetti
A Dark Protectors Novella

THE PROMISE OF SURRENDER by Liliana Hart
A MacKenzie Family Novella

FOREVER WICKED by Shayla Black
A Wicked Lovers Novella

CRIMSON TWILIGHT by Heather Graham
A Krewe of Hunters Novella

CAPTURED IN SURRENDER by Liliana Hart
A MacKenzie Family Novella

SILENT BITE: A SCANGUARDS WEDDING by Tina Folsom
A Scanguards Vampire Novella

DUNGEON GAMES by Lexi Blake
A Masters and Mercenaries Novella

AZAGOTH by Larissa Ione
A Demonica Novella

NEED YOU NOW by Lisa Renee Jones
A Shattered Promises Series Prelude

SHOW ME, BABY by Cherise Sinclair
A Masters of the Shadowlands Novella

ROPED IN by Lorelei James
A Blacktop Cowboys ® Novella

TEMPTED BY MIDNIGHT by Lara Adrian
A Midnight Breed Novella

THE FLAME by Christopher Rice
A Desire Exchange Novella

CARESS OF DARKNESS by Julie Kenner
A Dark Pleasures Novella

Also from Evil Eye Concepts:

TAME ME by J. Kenner
A Stark International Novella

THE SURRENDER GATE By Christopher Rice
A Desire Exchange Novel

SERVICING THE TARGET By Cherise Sinclair
A Masters of the Shadowlands Novel

Bundles:
BUNDLE ONE
Includes Forever Wicked by Shayla Black
Crimson Twilight by Heather Graham
Captured in Surrender by Liliana Hart
Silent Bite by Tina Folsom

BUNDLE TWO
Includes Dungeon Games by Lexi Blake
Azagoth by Larissa Ione
Need You Now by Lisa Renee Jones
Show My, Baby by Cherise Sinclair

BUNDLE THREE
Includes Roped In by Lorelei Jame
Tempted By Midnight by Lara Adrian
The Flame by Christopher Rice
Caress of Darkness by Julie Kenner

About Donna Grant

New York Times and USA Today bestselling author Donna Grant has been praised for her "totally addictive" and "unique and sensual" stories. She's the author of more than thirty novels spanning multiple genres of romance. Her latest acclaimed series, Dark Kings, features dragons, the Fae, and immortal Highlanders who are dark, dangerous, and irresistible.

She lives with her two children, three dogs, and four cats in Texas.

For more information about Donna, visit her website at www.DonnaGrant.com.

Passion Ignites
Dark Kings #7
By Donna Grant
Coming November 3, 2015

He consumed her with that kiss, leaving no question that whatever was happening between them was meant to be-that it had always been meant to be...

HE LOVES FOR ETERNITY

Thorn is the bad boy of the Dragon Kings, a gorgeous, reckless warrior whose passions run wild and fury knows no bounds. When he sees the brave, beautiful Lexi being lured into the Dark Fae's trap, he has no choice but to rescue her from a fate worse than death. But by saving this tempting mortal, he exposes himself to his fiercest enemy-and darkest desires. As the war between Dragons and Fae heats up, so does the passion between Lexi and Thorn. And when love is a battlefield, the heart takes no prisoners...

SHE LIVES FOR VENGEANCE

Lexi is on a mission of justice. Every day, she searches for the monster who murdered her friend. Every night, she hides in the shadows and plots her revenge. But the man she seeks is more dangerous than she ever imagined. He is one of the Dark Fae who preys on human life, who uses his unearthly power to seduce the innocent, and who is setting a trap just for her. Nothing can save Lexi from a creature like this-except the one man who's been watching her every move...

* * * *

For two weeks, Thorn had been in Edinburgh with Darius hunting the Dark Fae. He wasn't exactly thrilled that the Dragon Kings were spread so thin throughout Scotland to kill the bastards.

Then again, he was killing Dark Fae, which made him extremely happy.

He liked Darius, even if he had his own demons to battle. Darius wasn't the issue. It was Con.

Thorn halted his thoughts as he jumped from the roof he had been on and landed silently behind two Dark. He came up to them and smashed their heads together. Then, with his knife, he slashed their throats.

Both Fae fell without a sound. Damn, did he ever like his job. Thorn threw both Dark Fae over his shoulder and hurried to the warehouse where he and Darius were stashing the bodies.

He did most of his killing at night when the Dark came out to prey on the mortals, but Thorn never passed up an opportunity to kill the buggers.

There were half a dozen Dark laying dead in the warehouse. With merely a thought, he shifted, letting his body return to its rightful form—a dragon.

His long talons clicked on the concrete floor as he looked down at the Dark. Thorn inhaled deeply, fire rumbling in his throat. Then he released it, aiming at the bodies.

Dragon fire was the hottest thing on the realm. It disintegrated the Dark Fae bodies instantly. When there was nothing left but ash, Thorn shifted back into his human form.

He clothed himself and returned to the streets that were overrun with Dark. The humans had no idea who they were walking beside or having drinks with. Many mortals he and Darius had saved from being killed by the Dark, but there were so many more that they couldn't reach in time.

With just two Dragon Kings in the city against hundreds of Dark Fae, the odds were stacked against the humans.

Thorn didn't understand why the mortals couldn't sense how dangerous the Dark were. Or perhaps that's exactly what drew them to the Dark—that and their sexual vibes the humans couldn't ignore.

The Dark weren't as confident as they were a few weeks ago. Their ranks were dwindling, and though they suspected Dragon Kings were involved, they had yet to find him or Darius.

If two Dragon Kings could do so much damage, imagine what twelve could do? That brought a smile to Thorn's face. The Dark thought they were being smart, but they had begun the war a second time. And Thorn knew it would be impossible for the humans not to learn just what inhabited their realm with them.

His smile faded when his gaze snagged on a woman he had seen daily for the past week. She kept hidden, but it was obvious she was following the Dark.

She had a determined look on her face, one that had anger and revenge mixed together. Thorn knew that expression. It was the one that got mortals killed.

Her pale brown locks hung thick and straight to her shoulders. She tucked her hair behind her ear and peered around the corner of a store.

Thorn slid his gaze to the three Dark she was trailing. They were toying with her. They knew she was there.

"Damn," Thorn mumbled.

He and the other Dragon Kings vowed to protect the humans millions of years ago. They fought wars and sent their own dragons away to do just that. He couldn't stand there and let the Dark kill her.

Nor could he let them know he was there.

He flattened his lips when she stepped from her hiding spot and followed the Dark down the street. They were leading her to a secluded section.

Thorn didn't waste any time climbing to the roof of the building. He kept to the shadows and jumped from roof to roof as he tracked them.

He let out a thankful sigh when she ducked into an alley. Thorn jumped over the street to the opposite building before landing behind her.

"Not this time," he heard her say.

An American. Southern by her accent. He reached to tap her on the shoulder when his enhanced hearing picked up the Darks' conversation. They were coming for her.

Thorn wrapped a hand around her mouth and dragged her behind a Dumpster. "Be quiet and still if you doona want them to find you," he whispered in her ear.

She was struggling against him, but his words caused her to pause. A second later, she renewed her efforts.

Thorn held her tightly, her thin form easy to detain. The more she struggled, the more he could feel every curve of her body.

It wasn't until the Dark reached the alley that she stilled. He couldn't even feel her breathing.

"There's no one here," one of the Dark said in his Irish brogue.

"She was here."

The third snorted. "Not anymore. Come on."

A full minute passed before the three walked on. The woman's shoulders sagged as she blew out a breath. Thorn released her and held up his hands as she whirled around to face him.

Slate gray eyes glared at him with fury as her full lips pulled back in a scowl. Her cheekbones were high in her oval face.

She wasn't a great beauty, but there was something about her that wouldn't let Thorn look away.

"You're in way over your head," he told her.

On behalf of 1001 Dark Nights,
Liz Berry and M.J. Rose would like to thank ~

Steve Berry
Doug Scofield
Kim Guidroz
Jillian Stein
InkSlinger PR
Dan Slater
Asha Hossain
Chris Graham
Pamela Jamison
Jessica Johns
Dylan Stockton
Richard Blake
BookTrib After Dark
The Dinner Party Show
and Simon Lipskar